VITTORIA'S DIARY

BASED ON THE LIFE OF
VITTORIA GIULIANA D'ANTONIO

BY DAVID E. KETTLEWELL

Published by Motivational Press, Inc.
7777 N Wickham Rd, # 12-247
Melbourne, FL 32940
www.MotivationalPress.com

Copyright 2014 © by David E. Kettlewell

All Rights Reserved

No part of this book may be reproduced or transmitted in any form by any means: graphic, electronic, or mechanical, including photocopying, recording, taping or by any information storage or retrieval system without permission, in writing, from the authors, except for the inclusion of brief quotations in a review, article, book, or academic paper. The authors and publisher of this book and the associated materials have used their best efforts in preparing this material. The authors and publisher make no representations or warranties with respect to accuracy, applicability, fitness or completeness of the contents of this material. They disclaim any warranties expressed or implied, merchantability, or fitness for any particular purpose. The authors and publisher shall in no event be held liable for any loss or other damages, including but not limited to special, incidental, consequential, or other damages. If you have any questions or concerns, the advice of a competent professional should be sought.

Manufactured in the United States of America.

ISBN: 978-1-62865-151-5

Contents

Reflections In The Water 7
Dedication: 9

PART I

Birth 13
Death 16
The Piazza And Silvia's Store 17
The Diary 20
The Priest 22
Music And Girls 25
Gypsies 27
Anywhere There Is Gypsy, There Is Family 29
The Bicycle 31
Giuliana On Her Bicycle…Free 34
A Tall Blonde Soldier 36
Gypsy Ride 37
A Walk With Gennaro 38
Talk With Lea 41
That Night 42
Café The Next Night 44
The Dream 46
A Gypsy's Luscious Hair 47
Paradise 48
Talk Of The Convent School 49
The Walk 50
Inside The School 52
Gypsy Theft 56
Night 58
Sister Gena And Giuliana 62
Visitor 64
In Bed 66
Store 68
Sister Gena's Tears 70
Gypsy Fruit 72
The Beach At Giulianova 75
Dinner 78
Home 79
Lea And Sabatina In Evening 80

Gypsies… Paulo's Foul Mind	83
Gypsy Eyes	84
Light Tan Shoes	86
Vittoria's Diary	89
Words	91
Home	92
Giuliana's Brother Claudio	93
A Conversation With The Priest	95
Biagio's Journey	98
Giuliana's Figure	99
Washing Clothes	102
Silvia's Edict	104
In The Store	105
Love & Biagio's Mother	106
Cigarettes & Thieves	109
Love	112
Gay	115
Grape Festival	117
A Kiss At The Beach	123
Diary	125
Vince's Eyes	126
Watching	129
The Store	130
Missing The Boat	131
Fight	132
Losing The House	133
Vince's Dream	134
Night	135
The Beginning	136
The Deal In Giulianova	137
A Pleasant Start	139
Diary	140
Having To Wait Ten Years	141
Lea's Home	142
Lea's Talk With Silvia	143
Hammer	144
Guiliana Again Asks For A Garden	147
Vittoria's Diary	148
The Gypsy Tango	149
Room	151

Store Talk 152
Biagio's Mother At Lea's Home 153
Biagio Sick 155
Vittoria's Diary Entry 157
Friends 158
The Priest's Cottage 161
Gennaro And Silvia In Bed 162
Vince Asks…Marry Me 164
The Note To Giuliana And A Meeting 165
Hidden In Teramo 167
The Spring Of Discontent 168
Wedding Preparations 170
The Priest Tries Again 171
A Priest's Last Words 173
Spring 174
Gypsies…Attempted Rape 175
Old Friends 176
Gypsy Deal 177
Gypsy Dark Night 178
Morning 181
Love 182
Wedding Day 183
Evening 185
Love Nest 187
Diary 188
The Night Of Silvia 189

PART II

Time On Her Mind 193
Flight 195
Landing 198
Oasis 200
Giuliana's New Home 202
Morning 205
Lies 208
Diary 209
Dancing 210
Love And Money 211
Visit To Akron 212
Back 214

Diary 216
Argentina's Home 217
Giant Auto 218
Clock 221
Dancing In Ohio 222
The Diary…Pregnant 224
Sheets 225
Giuliana's First Son Michael 226
Darius's Kindness 228
Depression 230
Diary 231
Boat 232
The Two Oxen 233
Gypsies…Alvana's Truths 238
Giuliana 242
Back To Italy…A Thousand Clouds 244
Back To Sears 247
The Importance Of The Diary 248
Cuyahoga Falls Ohio 249
Dr. Nieman's Mercedes 250
Marco And Rita 251
I Am In Prison But Have Committed No Crime 252
The Anguish Of Years 253
Diary 254
Vince's Change 255
Dreams 256
Vince And His Children 257
Rita 258
Vince's Injury & West Point Market 259
The Wall—Giuliana's Letter To Vince 260
Vince's Illness 263
The Last Walk Through Mosciano Sant'angelo, Italy 264
Funeral 265
Mosciano 266
Diary 267
A Last Goodbye To Biagio 268
Honto's Death 270
The Rope To Heaven 271
Closure 273

REFLECTIONS IN THE WATER

Giuliana was beautiful as few women have been, 15, with a figure to equal Sophia Lauren.

Her legs pumped the bicycle madly as she rode through the Piazza in Mosciano Sant'Angelo, Italy, perched a few thousand feet above the Adriatic Sea.

Dressed in a full-cut light blue skirt with a blue and white striped top, she was the most beautiful woman in town.

The birds on the wire, (the retired men sitting in a row of chairs—each in the same seat each day, at one end of the Piazza) looked forward to her bicycle rides and her beauty and freshness as it reminded them of all those things which in steady progression had exited their lives with age, as they do for us all.

Young men saw her and dreamed of pressing their lips to hers, or more, while Giuliana's mother, Silvia; a small powerfully-built woman, worked in her small, cramped convenience shoppe selling pasta, cigarettes, and many small items in the Piazza.

The beautiful terra cotta bricks, and centuries-old buildings whirred by as she rode, and she breathed deep the fresh air and basked in the security one has in knowing each face you pass in a small town.

Scents of the flowers and fresh bread from the bakery entered her nostrils, she smiled, and the colors of the fruit in wooden crates spun by, and the small jeweled rings and necklaces in the shoppe windows too. From a bird's eye view all the small roads in the surrounding countryside led to this Piazza…the heart of life in Mosciano Sant'Angelo.

She saw glimpses of the Adriatic Sea as it sparkled, flat and calm, just 3 miles to the East through rolling hills, and then turned the bicycle West to see the Gran Sassos mountains in a grey blue mist ahead.

Her leg pirouetted off the bicycle, and she entered the store with a skip.

A man with his small sack of groceries from the store got on the bicycle which Giuliana had returned to him, then waved to her and rode slowly away, the front wheel see sawing, first one way, then the other, for balance.

All this was before she was sold into a marriage so her parents could buy a house, before she had her children in America with a man she did not choose, and before her true love for her childhood sweetheart Biagio would haunt her every waking moment.

Like a needle point, a woman's life is crafted stitch-by-stitch, and what we know of what lies ahead for us; who we will love, what we will gain, what we will lose, our fate as it will—what we know of it is nothing.

Dedication:

This book is dedicated to my departed mother, Barbara Kettlewell, (she was a writer) and to my dearest friend Vittoria Giuliana D'Antonio, whoever she truly is inside her heart which has endured so much, and to Marlene Czetli who has provided so much help.

PART I

BIRTH

Gennaro D'Antonio, slender and immaculately dressed in a tasteful suit with matching tie and his soft Spanish leather shoes he'd made by hand, sat in the stuffed chair of the bedroom of their home in Mosciano Sant'Angelo, with his trumpet.

He rubbed the perfectly formed brass tubes and valves over and over with his hand, like a lover caresses a woman, tapping the pearl valve keys, hearing them, tap tap tap.

"It shouldn't be long now," said Dr. Rinaldo with his gigantic almost circus-like moustache, as he peered under the sheet to view Silvia's, Gennaro's wife's, private parts one more time.

"The baby, it wants to come," said the doctor as he wiped his forehead with his handkerchief.

Looking out the window, Rinaldo saw the sun sparkling off the blue waters of the Adriatic Sea just a few miles to the East, which lay like a calm gem pond among the gently undulating hills dotted with stripes of blue-grey olive groves and the darker green grapes, broken only by an occasional simple dwelling of cream stucco and faded red and brown clay tiles on the roof.

Then walking to the opposite window in the third story room facing West, the doctor saw the rising foothills of the Gran Sassos mountains with their misty shades of grey and soft brown hues, which rising like a backbone divides Italy its entire length, and served as a barrier to invasions of armies West to East for centuries.

"Gennaro, this house has the best view in Mosciano, maybe the world…you are lucky."

The doctor had the beautiful rich golden skin and deep set satisfaction reflecting a life lived in a virtual paradise of warmth and delicious foods shared by most persons living in the small town of Mosciano Sant'Angelo, halfway down the leg of Italy just 3 miles from the Adriatic Sea.

The townspeople revered the town and loved the town as few in other places could imagine, as they sensed that theirs was perhaps the most lovely place on earth.

When aging relics such as the rounded fort tower facing the sea begin to crumble, the mortar failing at last after centuries of winter rains, workmen with dry cracked hands clean the bricks one by one, with the entire structure rebuilt exactly as originally designed. It was a world of reverence for the past and Italy's grand role in the march towards civilization. Each child knew of Rome and its historical prominence; they were the beginning of civilization and an argument could be made they knew more of living a satisfying life than most peoples.

Gennaro did not hear Rinaldo's words, as he was focused intently on the fast arpeggio of notes like a waterfall running uphill he had to perform later in the week.

"Perfetto, perfetto, your music must be perfetto…and the road is endless practice. Art is earned, not granted," whispered the voice of his dead father in his ears.

"Gennaro, why don't you wait in the next room, I'll call you," said Dr. Rinaldo as his hand slopped his wet hair over the top of his head to hide the baldness.

Silvia, now in some pain had heard the trumpet notes rise and fall from her husband in the next room through her own light screams, which now were more frequent as the doctor's hand massaged her labia and musculature inside to test its readiness to pass the child, and help her relax.

With sweat dripping on the pillow, she said, "My life is lived to the tempo of trumpet," then her tough, almost manly face contorted and she screamed as if a murder had taken place and another contraction began.

"A bit longer," said Dr. Rinaldo as he held her hand, looking at the softness and pleading in Silvia's eyes.

As he held and stroked her hand, he thought how a doctor often sees what others do not; for Silvia was *the little soldier.*

"Why do you laugh? At my pain?" said Silvia.

"Oh no, I'm thinking of how strong you are, but how gentle now."

"You mean you're thinking I'm pushy, like a bull, but not so pushy now," she said with a marksman's aim, laughing.

"I can't believe you're laughing," he said.

"This is a woman's fate—to laugh through unbearable pain," she answered as she peered at this balding harbinger of both life and death, as she thought of the similarities between herself and the doctor.

Turning away she said, "They don't know the cares of a woman who has to run a home. Music may feed a soul, but it doesn't feed a family," she intoned as she thought of all the work left undone in the last two days at her small shop in the Piazza, or town square just two blocks away.

Gennaro held the sweet smelling, moist baby in his arms, rolling her wet fingers in his over and over, and kissed her cheeks with the gentility of a priest. On the carpet lay his trumpet, the first time in its life it wasn't in the case when out of his hands.

"Vittoria, Vittoria, I am your father your whole life," he sang to her. "Here, take her again while I put my trumpet away," he said to his wife.

As he lifted the trumpet to place it in the blue velvet lined case, he put it to his lips and began to play.

The following day, Gennaro went to the City Hall to register the baby's name as Vittoria Giuliana D'Antonio.

When he returned home, he proudly showed his wife Silvia the certificate.

"Why did you do that?," she said in slight anger, "I wanted her name to be Giuliana Vittoria, not Vittoria Giuliana."

"I wanted her name to be Vittoria, we talked about it and agreed on it," he said.

"No, her name will be Giuliana, and that's that," said Silvia.

DEATH

20 days later…

The baby Vittoria's sister, MariaTeresa just 20 months old, had fought for life all night with a worsening intestinal infection, then congestion of the lungs…believed to be caused by an allergic reaction to a shot.

Choking breath with syrupy sputum gagged her with her condition steadily declining until Dr. Rinaldo had said what Silvia could not believe she'd heard…"I have to go, to help another patient who is very ill, I am sorry, but I do have to go," he said.

"You're just going to give up?" Silvia said in anger. Dr. Rinaldo looked at the floor.

"Please forgive me, there is only one doctor," he said, and left.

Twenty minutes later, Vittoria's sister lay still, enveloped in death in her bed.

Gennaro sat with his head drooping down staring at his shoes, concentrating on the short breaths he took as Silvia stood and walked quickly to her bedroom.

She entered the bedroom and threw herself face down on the embroidered white linen pillowcase and wept in halting hiccups, grabbing a clump of hair in her left hand which shook terribly, and tore much of the hair out of the left side of her head.

"Thank God I still have my first born son, William," she thought. She did not think or speak of Giuliana.

THE PIAZZA AND SILVIA'S STORE

The Piazza was the center and heart of Mosciano, like many of the Italian cities created centuries ago; a living, pulsating heart for the people and their daily lives.

The townspeople flowed into the Piazza each day to buy their fresh bread, by the whole or half loaf, with some prized peaches or grapes grown by local farmers on farms held for generations by the same family. Jewelry stores, book and magazine stores selling pastries and cappuccino, ice cream shoppes, professional offices, two fruit shops which competed ferociously with the fresh figs one day and peaches and grapes on sale another; all making a solid ring of retail activity housed in buildings on the whole built centuries before; buildings made by hand of bricks and mortar of subdued hues of terra cotta, pink-grey, or browns…an artwork in and of themselves.

And in the center of all these shoppes was the Piazza itself, an expanse of hand-laid stones large enough to hold the weekly market of traveling merchants and gypsies in temporary tented stalls selling all manner of shoes, clothing, foods, and roasted pig.

The Piazza was life…the flowing of people; people talking, people laughing, touching the items, or sipping cappuccino watching the others shop.

And it is this very close contact of people talking with other people, and enjoyment of people on a daily basis which is so much the heart of life in rural Italy, then and now.

In the same place every day sat the "birds on a wire," the retired men of distinction who sat in the exact same chairs at the far end of the Piazza to watch life flow by and comment on all.

It had been 14 men total, but Mr. Pernambuco died of a heart attack last year, so now it was 13.

"It was where you went to rest before you're put to rest," Pernambuco had said laughing, days before he fell on the stones in his home's garden.

"Teresa's daughter, she's getting a figure, she will be tall like her mother," said Chico, a retired barber.

"She will have a full figure like her mother…good for her," said Dr. Spitzi.

"Good for all of us," said Chico laughing as he rubbed the heel of his shoe into the stone walk.

They slapped their hands and laughed.

Some of the townspeople, especially the young men, looked a bit askance at the "birds on the wire," some even made jokes, but the older men knew that in time all these young men would join them…or take their places: just let day-by-day go by, and then it was a lifetime, then they would lay in eternity in the mausoleum on the high hills just outside of town overlooking the Adriatic Sea, with framed photographs marking their marble-faced spaces…and the closer you got to that day the more you sensed and knew its reality. For young men, the end of life had no meaning, but that too the birds on the wire enjoyed.

And in the Piazza at the preferred end, close to the residential homes behind, was Silvia and Gennaro's store, but everyone knew it as hers—as he was seldom there due to the many music rehearsals and the constant touring for performances with the orchestra.

The store was no bigger than a rich man's closet, jammed with the things we'd call "convenience store items" like a razor, milk, tobacco, candy, a drink, a can opener, a little bracelet, tins of coffee, for Silvia grasped before most that people would pay a premium for all these things, or for a silly pink child's umbrella as they walked by, if at hand's reach—especially if they enjoyed conversation.

She also knew that the larger part of her business was the constant flow of gossip, her own equivalent of her husband's music.

Who was pregnant by which boy (said in whispers), who was to go to college, whose Mama or Papa was close to death, when the overhang by the theatre damaged by heavy storm would be completed…such a loss to the town as it had the best view of the Adriatic Sea and was close to Caro…the coffee shop supposedly owned by a Baltic woman but rumored to be firmly in the hands of the gypsies.

As happened throughout Southern Italy, even today, everything shut down from one o'clock to four o'clock each day, providing time for all people to go home to their meal of first pasta—and there were many types of pasta from tiny pastina in broth to a thick noodle, then small serving of meat which might be fish, or veal, or chicken or rabbit, prepared simply and tastefully…without the sickeningly pungent sauces of the French, then fruit and homemade wine and then a nap or an afternoon of making love, depending on your age and disposition.

"Giuliana, get your things, we're going to the grocery store," said Silvia in a barking, hoarse voice.

They walked the aisles as the townspeople nodded to Silvia with her slightly bowed legs, their eyes falling on Giuliana; so beautiful even at 5 with her large brown eyes and porcelain skin.

"Mama, please, this candy for me?" said the little girl.

"No, I told you to stop bothering me. Your dead sister, MariaTeresa, never begged and bothered me like you," Silvia said with a coldness far beyond what anyone could have understood.

And then the words escaped from her mother's lips which were to haunt Giuliana the rest of her life, "You were born to make your sister die."

"You were born to make your sister die."

"You were born to make your sister die."

Giuliana did not ask for things in the store after that.

THE DIARY

Across the street from the front door of Giuliana's home lived Lea, dark haired and tall, one of Silvia's closest friends possessing a personality prized by many cultures as ideal…calm, loving, and forgiving, as so much of a woman's life is forgiving.

Giuliana did not skip or hop on her way to Lea's home as she was deeply troubled by her Mother's comment that she was born to make her sister die.

The words were not clear in her little mind. Their meaning eluded her.

She knew her mama and papa loved her, although her father never said those words, and actually her mother never said those words, but certainly they did love her, they must love her, she thought. Did not all parents love their children?

Lea saw her beautiful blonde hair and smiling face at the door, and opened it giving Giuliana a long hug with her arms squeezing the girl tight, and a kiss on her cheek, "So, how is my favorite little girl in the whole world today?"

Giuliana was silent.

Lea, childless, poured all a woman's love on the child, and every day, seeing Giuliana was another day to dote on the child. Lea was married to the town's bus driver, Sabatina; a well-read man who adored his wife and after 15 years of marriage still held her and touched her lovingly each night, kissing her lips gently one at a time, while her fingers coursed through his silvery hair.

Giuliana did not speak, but began looking at the figurines on the shelf, and getting down on her knees to crawl and see the rows of books in the shelf, rose to peer at the items on the wooden desk and saw a red leather-covered book with gold on the sides of each page… open.

"Oh Lea, what's this?," Giuliana asked, touching the paper with her finger.

"This is a diary, sweetheart. I write my secrets into the diary," and sitting Giuliana on her lap, Lea opened it and began reading, "My brother will come to visit in two months, it's a beautiful morning today after yesterday's rain. I miss my mother today."

"I don't understand," said Giuliana.

"A diary is a place where you put your secrets that you would never tell anyone, private things that you share with the diary, but perhaps might not want to actually say to others."

"Do you talk to the diary?" said Giuliana.

"Oh no, you write in it, like this," said Lea.

"I have a secret," Giuliana said.

"What secret sweetheart?" said Lea.

"My mama says I was born to make my sister die."

The shock to Lea was no different than if a boxer had punched her in the middle of her abdomen, leaving her breathless.

"Oh, Giuliana, I'm sure she did not say that; you must have misunderstood her sweetheart," she said with a mix of shock and dread, as she knew words like this in fact could escape the mouth of Giuliana's mother.

"Mama was at the store and I wanted candy and she said I shouldn't ask because I was born to make my sister die."

Lea held Giuliana in her arms, and took her to the rocking chair where she held the girl and rocked, stroking her and the tears Lea shed were hidden from the child, as they fell into Giuliana's hair…as Lea's pain on hearing was even greater than what the child endured.

THE PRIEST

Father Nicola, the new priest in Mosciano Sant'Angelo, was a short and slender young man of 23 who had had grown up on a farm near the city of Teramo, working the soil with his brothers every day, but no one in Mosciano looked down on him…they found his country ways comforting and the simplicity of his early life a reflection of the values of renunciation of worldly things.

He came from a family with three brothers, and his mother who had been very devout, had always hoped one of her sons would serve the church. She said his joining the priesthood was a vindication of her life as all she had came from the wellspring of God's grace.

She would hold young Nicola in her lap and read to him from scripture, and in some way all his life, even after his mother's death, every action related to his duties in the church evoked the feelings of love from his mother.

Which is not to say that Nicola was singular in his thinking about the Catholic Church; he had faith in the teachings of the church, but also tried to see the truth in other religions, which was not a position likely to find support among a grouping of priests.

His father had said that one thing can be true, and another can be true also, and that simple definition seemed correct to Nicola.

Other than suffering from occasional back pain, his life was a comfortable one, although few who saw his living quarters would agree.

His temporary home was in a small cottage adjacent to the catholic convent school for orphans a few minute's walk from the Piazza.

All the walls were a bland whitewash, with a single small crucifix on the wall and one table with three wooden chairs, a wash basin and pitcher, and a towel. Food came from the school next door. His bedroom was equally bare…a single bed with one small dresser with one drawer stuck closed, and a writing desk, again with a crucifix on the wall.

Lea knocked at the door of the cottage and he opened it.

"Thank you for taking time to see me Father, in your home," she said.

"No, no," he said holding her hand, "I should thank you. It's not really my home, it's part of the school…I just use it."

"Of course," said Lea.

He looked for the telltale signs of why she'd come: hands which might plead or a saddened face, or the anger he at times saw in visitors, always always coming with the hope that the waters to wash away the errors of mankind were in his hands.

He opened his palm at a chair, and they sat.

"There is a little girl who lives next door to me, her name is Giuliana. Her mother owns the little store in the Piazza, they sell tobacco and this and that."

"Yes, I think I know the store," he said.

"She is the one who had her second child, MariaTeresa, die at 20 months about 4 years ago, just after Giuliana was born."

"It was before my time," he said.

"The mother; she and I are friends, close friends, and I'm not sure I should even tell you this…the little girl was at my home yesterday and said her mother and she were at the grocery store and the girl asked for candy, and her mother told her, 'You were born to make your sister die.'"

"I couldn't sleep all last night, and I was chilled and shaking a little. I don't do that, but I was upset and my husband said maybe I should talk to you," Lea said.

"I'm glad you came to see me…what are you thinking, because I can tell you are concerned, and I'll guess you've been thinking," he said.

He'd found that oftentimes those who came to see him had already thought of some way to solve their problems, if he gave them the opportunity to share their views, and for this he was already well-received in the town which could be neutral to strangers.

"That you look after the child, just a little, and keep an eye on her."

"To keep an eye on her," he said repeating her exact words.

"And what is her name, again?" he asked.

"Giuliana," said Lea.

MUSIC AND GIRLS

Giuliana sat on the floor with her doll having two black button eyes and watched the toe of her father's shoe go up and down in perfect rhythm, like waves of the sea as the sounds of the trumpet filled the room like a wind full of brightly colored leaves on a fall day.

Gennaro's shoes were soft roughed tan leather, and like all the shoes he made, exquisite, as his father had been a revered cobbler.

She heard the notes rise and fall, then he'd stop and begin again, playing the same phrase of music over and over.

"Papa, why do you play the same thing over and over?" she said when he took one of his short breaks.

"Giuliana, it's not the same; each is a little bit different."

"They sound the same to me," she said.

"Ok, let's see, I will play this series of triplets for you and see what you hear."

"What's a triplet?" she asked.

"Three little notes together, and then some more three little notes together, and all together they make a sentence, a musical sentence," said the girl's father.

Then he played and she heard the little triplets.

"Listen to this next one," he said.

This time the little triplets sounded a bit different.

"You see, I have to decide, do I want the little notes in the triplets to sound distinct and separate, or make them all flow together."

"What do you think?" she asked.

"I think they should be a little apart, but not too much because I have to play with other people and they might get confused if I'm not there. So, I'll take a little bit of time from the last note of the triplet away, and they'll stand alone…but not too much alone."

"Papa, I want to play harmonica."

"What?," he said.

"I want to play an instrument, a harmonica," she said.

"No, music is not for girls, it's for men," he said.

"Why?" she asked, but there was no answer.

Silvia walked quickly into the room, "Giuliana, get up off the floor and sit on a chair," then to Gennaro, "I'm leaving for the store, keep her with you till you leave for rehearsal."

Then she reached down towards Giuliana, but instead of touching her daughter, patted the doll with her hand, "Be a good little doll. Do what Giuliana tells you, like a good little girl does," then she walked out.

GYPSIES

Honto, aged 53, sat at the kitchen table of their home on the outskirts of town, just beyond the cemetery. It was not a poor man's home, or a rich man's home, non-distinctive and unobtrusive in every way possible. It seemed to melt into the landscape, and stood out in no way in particular, except that it was home to a grouping of gypsies who were well-liked by their neighbors, as they never caused any trouble.

Next to Honto was a bottle of his favorite Spanish red wine and a fluted wine glass half full, as he stroked his graying moustache, looking at the little check marks made in pencil only he understood in a little black book which was worn with use and age.

It was his personal record of income from stolen jewelry in the territory he and his "family" controlled which extended almost to Teramo. In the gypsy world, family very seldom mean true blood family, but more a collection of individuals of like mind, for what is blood but a river of all gypsy peoples? The home was a bringing together of people who pledge their honor and loyalty to each other in a cold world which has treated gypsies like outcasts without rights or dignity for centuries.

He held the wine in his mouth and let the flavor flow on his tongue and palate, and found it pleasing, just as his father had done before him. He missed his father who had taught him so much, he smiled as he thought of his father's favorite words…"It is God's well, and we all drink at it," and, "Do not put your faith in treasures…yours or others'."

Honto would tell you his family was "clean," meaning they had no hand in the filthy drug business, and personally did no stealing, although they organized most all of it, and woe to the outside thief who they caught stealing, as their code of life was that never, for any reason, does a gypsy call the police.

This lesson was brought home to Alfardo on his first night in the paradise of Mosciano Sant'Angelo with its lovely weather and delicious foods, when new to Honto's house, he suggested Alvana, a more than attractive gypsy woman in her 20's he'd been eyeing, with slender figure and small, upright breasts, long hair, and a shortened brow above her warm dark eyes and lips, could make more money selling "bush" than her pleading to townsfolk with a photo of a child in her right hand and palm outstretched in which she had some coins.

Of course, it was not really a photograph of her child, she had no child—she was a good gypsy woman with morals who would not let a man have her until he'd promised her a life together.

Pise, who resembled a human bull with massive chest and arms with tattoos made by a black pen from a short stay in prison, threw his chair to the floor and grabbed Alfardo by the shirt which tore, slamming him into a wall with enough force to make Alfardo's nose run red.

"You will shut your face; Alvana is no whore, she is a good girl from a good gypsy family. You are in a decent gypsy home...say anything against her honor again and I will do many bad things to you, and then watch you buried alive in a place where no one and I mean no one will care, for eternity."

Then Pise grabbed Alfardo's crotch squeezing hard as Alfardo's face contorted in pain, "She's not for this, you know what I mean."

Pise slapped Alfardo's face, really just to be sure he was aware, and said, "Say it. Say you understand."

"I understand," said Alfardo.

A bowl of soup was placed in front of Alfardo by Honto's woman Guardia, as he watched a drip of blood fall off his nose into the steaming liquid.

"You'll feel better after you eat this," she said not unkindly, adding, "you'd better listen to what he says. He can be unreasonable."

ANYWHERE THERE IS GYPSY, THERE IS FAMILY

The Horn, that was the name he went by, had a limp and a scar on his cheek, and an unkempt scruffy looking beard of grey and white prickles. He drove the old and decaying farm truck which carried the stolen gold and jewelry north, hidden in a thermos bottle.

"I heard what you said last night about the girl; you're lucky you're alive, sometimes he loses control and goes too far."

Alfardo was quiet.

"His memory is not too good. Just watch yourself, especially what you say to the women, or the young girl. Guardia is boss at the house and she didn't like what you said," The Horn said as he passed a cigarette to Alfardo.

They bounced up and down almost like a roller coaster on the back road.

Alfardo was thinking that he was in trouble; would they kill him for what he'd said? They might, he knew that in soft lands the gypsies are often hardest.

The actual stealing was done by travelling workers, like Alfardo, just getting their start in the trade; men or women often in their 20's or early 30's, some in their teens, who were young and agile enough to get into an empty home quickly and get out.

And there were rules.

The words of the older man who'd taught him when he first arrived in Mosciano came to Alfardo, "Don't break the lock, just pick it, and don't damage anything in the house; don't break any glassware or tear up artwork…just go in like a professional, do your job, and leave things neat. And don't take all the jewelry; leave some, so it looks like they just lost it or a family member stole it."

"Who cares what I do?" Alfardo had asked the man, as he drew on a cigarette, *"it's my skin."*

"We care because the police, they're not going to do anything about small jewelry, but when you make things embarrassing for them, then they have to arrest somebody, but they'll have no idea who to arrest so they'll just pick one, and it will be us…Honto's family…that can't be."

"What if I get caught by the police?"

"That depends on which police catch you."

The Horn looked at Alfardo, "What are you thinking? If they wanted you dead you'd already be dead. Don't forget…they need you, and you're young! That's two good things."

He grasped Alfardo's cheek, like kindly grandfather might do, fondly, and gave it a light slap.

"Don't forget, anywhere there is gypsy, there is family."

THE BICYCLE

Father Nicola looked in the three quarter length mirror with the small crack in the lower right corner on one wall of his bedroom, as he put on his simple black robe and sash.

"Do we dress this way because we want to look different, to be apart from others…or for its simplicity?" he asked himself as he had many times.

There was a time when this dress was close to the style others wore in Europe; a long simple robe…priests being in black with a cloth sash, while others of greater means wore lighter colors, with the rich in colorful ornate robes…but that was centuries ago. Why had the church not amended its dress code to something more current?

He left the convent school, taking the route to the East which gave him a view of the Adriatic Sea visible between the rolling hills.

He remembered that as a child of 5 he sat in the back of the truck with his siblings while they sang and talked of the fields and the joy they would have at the sea, and their toes in the hot sand. He remembered the softness of the salt water on his skin and his great disappointment one year when their annual trip ended abruptly as a storm came in from the Balkans.

And he remembered his one prayer to God on where he would be sent; "Dear God, if it is possible, put me by the sea. I know it is a selfish request, but I will ask it anyway."

As he stepped around a broken stone on the walk he thought, "I could have been a naturalist. Galileo almost chose to be a Priest; I wonder why he chose science and studying the stars? And why did the church place him under house arrest when all he did was speak the truth?"

He turned towards the Piazza then entered the round church made of pinkish and tan brick, and going to the two rows of candles where people could say a prayer, light a candle and place coins in the slot, he used a small key to open the coin box and put the coins and a few bills into a cloth pouch in his robe.

"This is your little oasis, use the money as you desire…everyone needs a few coins for this and that," the priest had told him his third day in training.

He walked the Piazza slowly for at every few steps someone would stop to talk: A death in a family; a new job; a question about a wedding date; a baptism; a problem they needed to talk about…people flowed to the priest like a gentle trickle of water from a rock face.

Yes, this was it; the small store selling tobacco and such. The father plays trumpet in the orchestra, and the little girl's mother; the one who runs the store, is Silvia. She attended church often, he less so.

"Good morning, Silvia," he said gently as he saw her finish up with a customer.

"I'll have that for you next week, I have to order it for you special," Silvia said as she handed a small package with coffee to the woman.

"You're probably right about the boy, his family does not come from money…good to know," the woman said as she nodded to the priest and left.

"Good morning, Silvia," the priest repeated.

"Maybe you want to make my store part of your church?" she said laughing, "I don't think I've ever seen you in here before."

"No, I like the store, so many things. I was thinking it would be nice for us to visit and get to know one another better."

"Oh yes," said Silvia, eyeing him.

"Well why don't you pick a day and let me know. We'll just visit and get to know one another better," he said.

"I would love that," said Silvia with a sour look on her face.

From the back of the store came Giuliana, and the priest thought she was perhaps the prettiest little girl he'd ever seen, with large eyes and flowing blonde locks.

"Not in school today?" asked the priest.

"No, I'm taking her to the doctor at noon," said Silvia.

Thomaso, a retired teacher with a limp from an auto accident entered, "Where's my little bicycle thief?," he said to Giuliana as she ran out the store, kicked up the kickstand and ran two steps with the bike, planted her foot on one pedal in its down stroke, and was off like a miniature racer.

"She always loves to ride my bicycle, she'll be back by the time I'm done," said Thomaso.

"I tell her to leave the bicycles alone," said Silvia.

"She doesn't need to ask me to ride the bike, I know her heart," said Thomaso, who was well loved by all in town as he'd taught most every adult at one time or another and was known for his kind and gentle ways with all.

The priest, Nicola, stepped outside and looked at the little girl on the bicycle, and he stood watching, he imagined her delight…and experienced it as his own delight, almost as if he were a child again.

David E. Kettlewell

GIULIANA ON HER BICYCLE...FREE

Giuliana skipped along with the bicycle, placed her left foot on the pedal on its down-stroke, threw her leg over the bicycle, and she was off!

Her little hips see sawed back and forth, as she was too small to actually sit on the seat, and had to straddle the top tube of the frame.

Her smile blossomed as she felt the wind on her face as she passed each of the shoppes, and her smile grew and grew until all her teeth glittered white and her eyes came alive as a bird in flight.

On she went; past the bank at one end, then past the flower vendor, and the long side of the Piazza with the coffee shoppe and the ice cream shop.

"Giuliana, whose bike have you got now? Don't go too fast," said a woman with a broom who looked up to see her pass, remembering her own childhood as she swept.

She weaved the bicycle in and out and around the tables like a skier might when decending a downhill race course and pumped the pedals harder…then coasted, hearing only the slight whirr of the wheels.

Thomaso waited for her to come to him with his bicycle, laughing.

"Well, my mechanic, what do you think of my bicycle today, does it meet with your approval?"

"Of course, I like your bike…your bike and I are best friends!" Giuliana answered.

The man tousled her hair with his right hand and then climbed on the bicycle holding his bag of items and rode off, after veering right when he lost his balance then and regained it with a twist of the handlbars.

The priest watched Giuliana silently as she went back into the store. He stood motionless, listening.

Silvia said in a hard voice, "Why did you take his bicycle? Didn't I tell you not to take his bicycle? Your sister MariaTeresa would not have taken that bicycle, she did what she was told, and walked to get me groceries every day. She was a good girl, not like you."

Which seemed odd to the priest's mind as he knew that Silvia's first daughter MariaTeresa had died when just 20 months old.

A TALL BLONDE SOLDIER

No bombs fell in Mosciano Sant'Angelo, Italy, during the war. The Italians argued about Mussolini, then argued about how to get rid of the Germans.

"We will be lucky to get out of here alive," said the Captain with the eye patch to the tall blonde solider from Northern Italy.

"We don't have to fear the Americans," said the soldier.

"It's the Germans, you fool. They'll kill us all if they can," said the Captain, "They won't leave without a nasty fight all along the road North, paved with our blood."

The tall soldier looked for Giuliana that day, as he did every day, and knocked at the door of the family's home.

Giuliana reminded him of his own daughter and he would bring her a gift of candy and ask how she was each day. There was a longing in his eyes, as if Giuliana represented all he had left behind for this accursed war…this war, this death, for what?

His hand would touch her curls, and he said, "When you are older, will you go to Northern Italy and think of me?"

One day after some bombs fell on a nearby town, he was gone.

They never heard if he was killed or survived.

GYPSY RIDE

Alfardo bounced and jerked as the truck driven by the older gypsy, The Horn, came to a desolate grape farm; run down, with trash and odd bits of rusting machines strewn about.

"It's a shame, this place could be cleaned up," said Alfardo to The Horn.

"To each their own," replied The Horn.

Out of the house with its faded and peeling paint and dirty windows came Paulo, a young man in his twenties with black hair slicked-back and a small moustache; a sickly stub of an upstart desperately wanting to be seen as a man.

"Up front, or in the back?," Paulo asked in his high-pitched voice.

"With us," said The Horn.

As he slid over to make room for Paulo, Alfardo glanced up at a second story window with no curtains in the house. A woman with her breasts just visible from an open nightgown peered down on them.

"For you," said Paulo to The Horn, as Paulo handed a metal lighter to the older man.

"Nice," said The Horn as he flipped the silver top with his thumb, and spun the wheel. Flame emerged, and he snapped the lighter shut.

"Where did you get this?," asked The Horn.

"It's for you," said Paulo as he laughed in his high-pitched giggle.

David E. Kettlewell

A WALK WITH GENNARO

"I'll take her for a walk so you can visit with the priest," said Gennaro to his wife, as he took Giuliana by the hand and walked out the door of their home together.

"Are we going to practice music later?" asked Giuliana, as her favorite time each day was listening to her father play his trumpet.

She would lie on the floor with her doll, letting the doll be the conductor: lifting and lowering her doll's arm to accompany her father's rapidly rising musical arpeggios, and then the fall of the notes which made one feel that water was being poured out of a china pitcher.

Not one person in Mosciano had a bad word regarding Gennaro; from his father's shop as a cobbler, and a respected one at that, Gennaro had risen to become the finest trumpet player in the region.

"See, talent runs in the family," people said.

Crowds came to hear him play with the orchestra, some coming from nearby towns, and the programs often ended with a long solo where he displayed his technical and artistic mastery of his instrument.

With not one enemy in the town, he was like honey in that he drew attention and even a form of adoration from all, with a reputation for a working man's patience and respect for everyone.

"Gennaro, Gennaro, please wait up," called out a man with a cane who saw the father and daughter.

Giovanni, with his stubble beard and cap; a retired policeman, came up and kissed Gennaro on both cheeks, and touched Giuliana's lovely curls with his aging and spotted knuckled hands.

"So, I heard your program last night, and I think it was one of your best. Sometimes I think I hear the voice of God in your playing."

"That's the kindest thing anyone has said of my playing, how kind of you," said Gennaro, as he placed his hand on Giovanni's shoulder. Gennaro could feel the thinness and angularity of the man's body under his suit.

"And so, what instrument is it to be for your beautiful daughter?" asked Giovanni.

Gennaro could not answer as two ladies joined the group. They touched Giuliana, commented on her beauty, and told Gennaro of their plan to visit Silvia later in the day at the shoppe, and something about a perfume they wanted her to find for them.

Later that day…

The priest came to the home of Silvia and Gennaro, but was greeted by Silvia alone. She had been watching out the curtain for him.

"How good to see you, Father, and how nice you came to visit," said Silvia, "what a shame I don't have the time I'd like, as I'm leaving for the store soon."

"I won't stay long," Father Nicola said. She led them into the kitchen where a bowl of green and dark red grapes awaited.

They sat and he began.

"I know you don't have much time. I came because I wanted to talk with you about your loss of your daughter."

"I already talked to the other priest about that," she said as she slid a small white plate to the priest for the seeds from the grapes.

"I would imagine it was hard for you," the priest said.

"Death is always hard," she replied.

"And how are things with your daughter?"

"Giuliana? She's not a problem," said Silvia.

"Do the two of you spend time together doing things?" he asked.

"Father, my husband is a fine musician, but the house and the food come from the store which I run every day. She comes and sits with me while I work."

Silvia stood and walked to the cupboard for a glass of water.

The priest was saddened by her answer, as he could hear in her voice and see in the home that there was little in the way of kindness and love for the girl here…as the women in town had told him many times in strict confidence.

He tried to think of a gentle way to ask Silvia if she loved the child, and why she had blamed Giuliana for the death of her sister, MariaTeresa at 20 months, but he could not find the words, although he had prayed for some way to open that door.

He also remembered the advice of a mentor that one rarely knows what is in the heart of another, for people seldom speak of their inner truths; being afraid and ashamed…but prefer to couch their feelings in anger towards others, or gossip.

The house reminded him of a short children's story he'd read once called, "The Invisible Girl," about a child who the parents could neither see, nor speak to, and then it came to him.

"I was thinking," said Nicola, "I can imagine your life is so busy here and you bear so much responsibility, perhaps you might want to place Giuliana with us at the school."

"Your school is for orphans," Silvia said eyeing him, "and we have no money for a private education."

"We have a fund for children, and we may be able to provide her with a place to stay with the other children. It's an excellent school," he said.

"When would we see her?," asked Silvia, as she stared at him the way she might when a fine bargain was offered, *as her father had said, "When someone offers a gift…accept it."*

"Whenever you like, she could come home every night, or come home on weekends, you decide."

TALK WITH LEA

"That's good news that the store is doing well, Silvia," said Lea as she put the finely ground coffee into the small percolator to make cappuccino.

Silvia began, "I'm busy enough, and I can't count on my husband to help, you know men, great interest in their own interests, but not so much the day-to-day of a home."

Then Silvia added, "I'm thinking of putting Giuliana in the convent school, she's always underfoot."

"Don't go there again," said Lea as she watched her friend's face.

"The priest said Giuliana could go to the convent school, I'm tempted," said Silvia.

Lea was so shocked she couldn't really speak and her hand began to tremble as she lifted the cappuccino pot, spilling water, then went to the sink and ran cool water on her hands, collecting herself.

Lea watched as the water swirled past her fingers and disappeared down the drain.

THAT NIGHT

Giuliana was sleeping, and Gennaro read the newspaper intently.

Gennaro said little as Silvia knitted, then putting down the paper and taking her arm, the two climbed the stairs to their bedroom.

He lay in bed next to his wife thinking of how to bring up the topic.

"Explain again to me what you're thinking about the school," he said.

"I told you. The priest says Giuliana can go to the school. It's a good school and we won't have to pay. Money's tight and it's one less mouth to feed."

"And?"

"And I don't want her underfoot; it's too much," said Silvia, adding, "She will be at the school and will receive the best education possible."

"And you're wrong about what you said today…not everyone who goes there is an orphan," said Silvia, her temper rising.

"Then let's bring her home at night," said Gennaro.

"She comes home on Sundays," said Silvia.

And now Gennaro knew he was entering dangerous territory, as Silvia had stated her views.

He pleaded, "But Giuliana is our child…she needs our love too, she's only 5, can't she help at the shoppe?"

Silence.

Then he added, "I don't know where you got the idea that Giuliana was responsible for the death of MariaTeresa. Giuliana was just a baby."

"It's just too much…too much all at one time…caring for a sick child, caring for a baby. Giuliana gets underfoot. How would you understand, you are busy with your music, your travel; you are gone…this is something I have to do and I run the house; that's our agreement…the agreement that makes music the most important thing in your life…or did you forget that?"

Silvia was right; their agreement was that all in the household was in her control, but that control had increased over the years to where she decided everything—other than his music.

He had sacrificed so much to his music; the hours practicing, playing with other children, a lost childhood, now control of his own home, but this—asking his daughter to leave the house seemed too far a reach for him.

He was angry, but did not have the courage to tell his wife what he thought, and besides, what difference did it make to talk? She had made her decision and that was that…they would all have to live with her decision.

There was no other option.

And so he lay next to his wife, listening to her soft snoring, unable to sleep. Then, as he had done so many times to calm himself, he thought of a Bach piece, and in time drifted off.

CAFÉ THE NEXT NIGHT

"I don't know what to do. Now she has it in her mind to send Giuliana away to the convent school for orphans," said Gennaro to his close friend, Bertonio.

Bertonio played trombone in the orchestra; tall and slender and attractive. They'd been friends since the age of 5.

"She's a Grilli, what are you going to do?" said Bertonio.

"It doesn't matter what I do or what I say, Silvia gets it in her mind…something…and she won't let it go," said Gennaro.

"Like I said, she's a Grilli," said Bertonio. "For everybody, there are things in life you like, and things you don't like; things you can change, and things you can't."

Seeing this did not help, Bertonio took another path, for he was determined to comfort his boyhood friend, "And there is another side too…her side of things. Maybe it is too much for Silvia, and she does a good job at the shoppe, and she helps pay the bills…she's a good wife, better than most, yes?"

Gennaro nodded his assent.

"Look on the bright side," Bertonio added, "Giuliana will receive a wonderful education, and close to home. Many wealthy families send their children to private catholic schools…so it's like you're a wealthy man! Maybe it's not a bad thing…how can you tell? And she's a beautiful girl; her life will be easy, always. You and I know that," he said with a smile.

Gennaro said, "But you and I both know it doesn't matter what you say or what I say, Silvia has spoken and her words are like a rock."

"She may be a rock, but you are like water, maybe you can wear her down, bit by bit," said Bertonio.

"It would take centuries, I don't have that time. No. She will have her way—that much I know," said Gennaro, staring at his shoes, twisting them this way and that.

Seeing his friend distraught, he put his hand on Gennaro's shoulder. "We all have our burdens, perhaps this is a light one. If you want to share a bed with a woman, you have no choice but to do as she asks. And my friend, you do have a wife, and children, some do not."

And these words did comfort Gennaro. He nodded and raised his eyes as both Gennaro and Bertonio looked up at the stars and tasted the light breeze off the Adriatic.

"Mosciano is as close to heaven as God has made on earth," thought Bertonio, as he fought back tears remembering the death of his wife two years ago, and the powerlessness he felt as she became weaker and weaker each day. And then…she was gone.

THE DREAM

Giuliana, now age 6, began to have nightmares which would leave her wet upon wakening.

In one, she lived in the cemetery and had food bowls, a fork, and a glass for water in a concrete space just big enough for a child to sit in, set among other concrete spaces.

She could see the Adriatic Sea in the distance, but when she spoke, no words came out, but she could hear one bird chirping on a tree, but the tree was purple.

She did not understand the dreams, but came to fear them, and a feeling of dread would come over her afterwards.

She saw the priest one day in town. He saw her and tousled her hair with his hand, "And how is my little Giuliana today?"

"I have a secret," she said.

He knelt on one knee and looked into her eyes, "And what secret is that?" he said holding her hand lightly.

She told him of the dream.

He said, "We all have dreams but none of us know what they mean. Don't worry yourself over it…everything will work out…you'll see."

The priest walked back to the convent school brusquely, and did something he had not done for years, he cursed, "Mother of Christ," three times and looking down, he saw his hands were both shaking.

A GYPSY'S LUSCIOUS HAIR

Alvana knelt naked in the tub in the bathroom of the gypsy house, enjoying the feeling of warm water on her flesh.

She took the pitcher of water and dipped it in the water in the tub, pouring it over her long black hair and down her naked body.

Alfardo's (the young thief's) voice could be heard in the hall laughing, and then he burst in.

She saw his eyes course her body inch by inch as he stared fixated at her small rounded breasts with protruding nipples.

He stood with his mouth open, frozen.

Instead of screaming at him, which she knew would cause him trouble as he was already in some trouble in the home due to his various stupid acts, she filled the pitcher again with water and raising her arms with the pitcher over her head, and with elbows spread open, turned her torso slightly towards him and let the water pour over her hair which then coursed down past her breasts, splashing into the tub…presenting her naked body to him openly…almost as if he were not there.

While Alfardo played the tough, there was much in him that was immature and childish, and that same naïveté had actually protected him from the gypsys' wrath more than he knew.

The truth was that while he told filthy jokes among his peers and bragged of many conquests, he'd never seen a naked woman before, or never a youthful lovely woman like Alvana.

He closed the door quietly and walked to the kitchen.

He was quiet the entire night, ate very little and fell deep into his own thoughts, and in his dreams he joined Alvana in the tub, but he was not washing her hair.

PARADISE

Giuliana had asked hundreds of times, or maybe thousands of times, it felt like forever.

It was Tuesday night, and her father was dressed in a light blue suit with light tan leather shoes and a white fedora hat. He looked for his glasses.

"Papa, can I go see the movie with you tonight? Please, please, please, I will do anything if I can just go to the movies with you."

He turned to her, "I'd already decided to take you, and now you've spoiled my surprise," he told her.

"Get a sweater and anything else you need, but quick, it starts soon," he told his daughter.

He held her hand as they walked to the theatre, and bought her popcorn and a soft drink, and she heard the laughter of the audience, but mostly she looked up at her father during the movie and played with the ring on his right hand, twirling it around and around his finger.

"This is what happiness is: you want something so long, and then you get it!" she thought.

TALK OF THE CONVENT SCHOOL

"We've decided that you are going to go to the lovely catholic convent school, and it's perfect because you'll get the best education," said Silvia as she knitted on the couch.

Giuliana was on her knees on the floor with her body draped over the couch looking first at her mother, and then at her father sitting in a chair fidgeting with the trumpet in his hands.

"I don't understand," said Giuliana, "did I do something to make you mad at me? I won't ask for candy any more at the store."

Giuliana looked at her father but he just stared at the floor, and did not make eye contact.

Many things went through Giuliana's mind; she'd seen the school, but thought everyone there was an orphan. Nobody in town went there, all the children went to the public schools.

"It's for orphans," Giuliana said softly.

"No, others go there too," said her mother, "I'm sure you'll like it very much and we will see you on Sundays, all day," said her mother.

"I don't understand," said Giuliana as her father got up and went to the kitchen.

The mother continued, "You go to school there every day, sleep there, and then on Sundays you come home."

"But I can walk home in 5 minutes, I can walk alone, you don't even have to come and get me—I can walk that far," pleaded Giuliana.

What going to the convent school would mean, exactly, Giuliana did not know, but she did know her mother well, and she knew that there were no words she could say that would change her mother's mind, and that there was little use in talking about it.

Giuliana looked at her father many times that night, but his gaze was always elsewhere. He did not practice trumpet that night, but went to bed early.

THE WALK

Lea put the small grouping of Giuliana's clothes including her little light blue sweater with the rhinestones decorating the front, socks, underwear, and one extra pair of shoes into the canvas-covered suitcase.

"Don't worry sweetheart," Lea said to Giuliana, "I'll bring over anything else you need, and I think I can come every day for a while to spend time with you and get to know all the wonderful people at the school."

"Let's finish up, your mother will be here any moment," Lea said as she went back and forth from the closet to the suitcase, then through the drawers, then back to the closet again in a disjointed way which made Giuliana uncomfortable, or maybe the child's fears affected Lea. Who could know?

"The blue or the red blouse?" Lea thought, but she could find no answer.

Then Lea sat by Giuliana on the bed and stroked the lobes of her ears and kissed her on her little red lips. "You know I love you, and so do your mama and papa. You'll get the best education and be close to home too, so everything is really best. It will be best, you'll see."

The only comfort Lea could find in this sea of sadness was that this was better than Silvia telling the child she'd been born to make her sister die… it was simply too much.

Giuliana could not speak. She tried to say words, but nothing came out. She had a far away look on her face, akin to what someone might look like were they banished from England to an Australian prison for a crime they did not commit.

Her emotions were somehow disconnected with her mind.

They heard Silvia come into the house, and her "hello."

"I don't have much time," said Silvia, as she kissed Lea.

The mother and daughter walked out the door of the house together, with Silvia carrying the suitcase and leading Giuliana by the hand.

"Don't dawdle back," said Silvia, tugging at the little girl's hand.

Then Giuliana began to cry very softly, and the mother tugged harder.

In this way they passed through the Piazza, and the older men, the birds on the wire…watched the two go by.

"Damn Grilli," said one.

"Hush, just be quiet, Gennaro might hear of it," another intoned.

With that they sat silent.

Giuliana could hear her shoes tapping on the bricks, and wished she could escape, but where?

"Why can't I come home every night," she asked her mother.

"You'll see, you'll love it there," Silvia said, as they went up the circular drive to the mansion which was to be her home and school.

It was massive, an estate really with a huge backyard overlooking the mountains and a garage with room for 5 cars to one side, which was now a storage area.

Giuliana's mind was full of so many thoughts, but she said nothing, like the time her mother said she was born to make her sister die, and she said nothing.

And the emotions inside that child would fill the Adriatic Sea.

INSIDE THE SCHOOL

The actual convent school was a home so large and ornate that Giuliana thought for a moment it was a castle she'd seen in a book.

The semi-circular driveway led with a slight rise to the front of the grand home, and it was much higher and larger than any home the little girl had seen. It seemed to rise to the sky itself as she looked up, and had a view of much of the countryside all around.

The brick was a very light brown, and the two front doors at the top of the semi-circular steps were ornately carved of dark wood.

Silvia pulled a chain and a small bell rang inside the school.

"A very rich man, an important man and his wife lived here, and they donated it to the church. Isn't it lovely? And look, it has two stories and look at the arch over the doors," said Silvia.

Giuliana said nothing, and Silvia tightened her grip on the child's hand.

The door opened and a very short woman in a black habit, maybe no more than four foot six stuck her head through.

"This is Giuliana D'Antonio," said Silvia, "I am her mother."

"My name is Sister Gena , and I am the door keeper among other things, actually…many other things," the little nun said laughing. She did not need to stoop down to look into Giuliana's eyes, as both the nun and the little girl were fairly close in height.

"You see I'm a good fit for my job," she said giggling, "a good and proper fit, as I say."

"I'm very glad to have a good little girl like you, because we already have enough naughty girls who don't understand rules!" she said bursting out in giggles again.

"Well anyway, you look like a good little girl, but we'll see what we see in the pudding," said Sister Gena.

Seeing she was not understood, Sister Gena added, "I meant we'll see what a wonderful little girl you are, and how well-behaved."

Then she turned and Silvia and Giuliana followed her inside.

Giuliana could scarcely believe what she saw on the inside of the home. They stepped into a large room and sitting at a desk directly in front of them was a nun dressed in a full habit with a white hat that spread almost two feet in width. She held papers in her hand and did not smile.

There was a chapel to the left, looking just like a little church with pews and figurines inset in the wall as a church would have.

Looking up from the main room the ceiling climbed and climbed far overhead to a second floor, and a banister flowed down to just behind the nun at the table.

The nun rose from her desk and walked to Giuliana…Sister Gena slipped away.

"So, we have a new student. I am Sarna, and how nice for you that you have parents who love you so much they put you into this marvelous school, you are a very lucky little girl, and I hope you will act accordingly. Obedience is a great virtue, for us all."

"Say Sarna," said the nun to the little girl.

"Sarna," answered Giuliana.

Giuliana was fascinated to see Sarna walk, because her huge black skirt seemed to flow over the floor, but she didn't really see any shoes or legs moving at all, it was like a doll which you might push with your hand along the floor.

"We have our own chapel as you see," said the nun, "and we have our own services as we have our own priest in the cottage, who you already know I believe," she said staring at Giuliana.

Giuliana nodded.

Sarna led them past the desk to a large private room with tables to the right, "We eat here, and behind and through this door is our kitchen," she said.

Giuliana did not remember seeing a kitchen so large in her entire life.

"Where are the children?" asked Silvia.

"Today is a special treat and they are at the beach in Giulianova for the day, with lunch prepared in baskets; all fresh foods," said Sarna nodding to Silvia.

Slowly they ascended the stairs, and found door after door with small rooms.

"This is yours," she said pointing to a room through a narrow door, with three beds.

"Why are there three beds?" asked Giuliana.

"Oh, Giuliana, they want you to have friends," said Silvia.

Sarna cut her off curtly, "There are no private rooms here. You will share your room and I've been careful to see that you will have good companions, not troublemakers."

Then Sarna added, "I know this is different for you, but you will adapt and be very happy here. Everyone is happy here."

"Why can't I come home every night?" asked Giuliana, looking up at her mother.

Sarna looked to Silvia as if to ask, "Haven't you told her?"

The nun stood silent a moment, then Silvia spoke.

"Giuliana, you will stay here during the week and on Saturday because the girls have so much fun together, and everyone likes to be together, and on Sundays I'll come and walk with you home and you can be with us during the day," said Silvia, giving Giuliana a hug which the little girl returned reluctantly.

"I want to sleep at home," Giuliana said as she started to cry.

Silvia hugged her daughter and whispered something in her ear.

Sarna turned back to Giuliana, "Getting along with me is easy, just do the best you can and don't create trouble."

On her way home, Silvia thought, "It's a good school and she will get a good education, a better education than otherwise."

And for some reason she could not explain, images of her dead child Maria Teresa came to Silvia over and over as she walked, until she had to sit on a stone bench by the round church and compose herself.

GYPSY THEFT

Alfardo could not remember when he had been more excited—he'd been staking out the house for 3 weeks and knew the patterns of the homeowners well.

It was a simple two-story stucco home with a nice view towards the Adriatic Sea, although only a very small patch of water could be seen, and no dog.

The windows had the strong storm shutters which locked, but his lock picking skills were excellent.

"They're not filthy rich, but they are not poor either," he thought as he crouched behind a grouping of bushes, waiting for sunset to end.

Honcho, the head of the gypsy family had told him, "Go in quickly; take some things…but not everything. Leave a bit of gold and jewelry so it looks like a family member took it, and don't break anything."

"If you carry a knife or gun, or hurt anyone, the family will not stand behind you and you will go to jail, and I don't have to remind you what the life of a gypsy is in jail."

"If no one is hurt…we can do many things to help you. Use your head, and do a good job, I think you'll do good…don't let me down. This is your first test."

Alfardo hid in the bushes until it was dark, looking at the view to the East and the tiny patch of the Adriatic Sea. "This is like the life of the gypsy," he thought, "I can see the beauty of the Adriatic Sea, but cannot touch it."

He inserted the two lock picking tools into the lock on the shutter facing the sea where no one could see him, and it opened easily. He turned to look at the view, "This is the kind of house I would like someday," he thought…"nice, but not too nice to raise questions."

He ran like a young deer up to the largest bedroom.

He walked to the woman's dresser and opened the jewelry box with its heavy wooden cover and drawers, then took out his leather sack and put a sapphire ring in, then a gold chain, then two gold rings. But in the lower tray he found more ornate rings, so put the two gold rings back, and took the jeweled ones.

"I like these better, they are pleasing to me."

For a moment he dreamed that he was in this bedroom with Alvana, and giving her the ring and she removed her clothes, and…

He went through the drawers quickly and was leaving the room, then stopped at the door.

"God, thank you for giving me these jewels; these people had more than they need. Maybe they will value what is left more now that I have some," and then he heard a pounding at the front door and he began to sweat profusely.

He did not want to look to see who it was, better to just stay put. He lay on the floor. The pounding on the door continued.

Then he heard a car door close and an engine start. "Why didn't I hear the car pull in?" he thought, "What are they doing?"

He was so frightened he shook uncontrollably, and went downstairs where he saw some small pictures on the mantle; one of a very beautiful young woman with long dark hair, with the look of a princess who has been given everything all her life.

And then he did something that he never understood.

He took the picture, placing it in his pocket, and left, closing and re-locking the shutter in the back, and was gone into the night.

NIGHT

That night, he lay in bed thinking of the congratulations accorded him by the entire family. Honto had a drink ready and Guardia was laughing, saying he was a good boy after all. Alvana had looked at him with a peculiar smirk and licked her lips.

He was just falling to sleep when Pise the bull came in and slapped his face hard.

"Honto wants to see you, now," and Pise shoved him against the wall and the door and anything they passed on their walk to the kitchen, where Honto and Guardia behind him waited with an empty chair.

"You should cut off his balls," said Honto.

"I had dinner late, we should cut his balls off tomorrow when I've digested my food," said Pise.

Pise shoved his hands down Alfardo's pants and grabbed Alfardo's balls squeezing them hard, "Well, they are still there and I don't suppose they will go anywhere," he said slapping Alfardo again.

"Let him talk," said Guardia as she studied Alfardo's face carefully.

"Is there something you want to tell me?" asked Honto at the head of the kitchen table as he peeled an apple, placing the rind in one bowl, and the flesh in another smaller bowl as he poured on olive oil, then sprinkled all with salt and pepper.

"No, nothing, I did what you asked me to do," said Alfardo. "I didn't break anything, and I left some jewelry so the police would think it could have been a family member or friend who stole, just like you told me."

"Yes, that's true, but that's not the whole truth, is it my lying Alfardo," said Honto as he put the knife into the apple piece and put it to his mouth. "It seems you have an interest in family photos. Isn't that so?"

Alvana walked into the room and placed the framed picture of the girl on the kitchen table by Honto.

"Explain yourself," said Honto.

Alfardo looked at the picture and hung his head, he opened his mouth and no words came out.

Guardia pushed everyone out of the room except Honto and Alfardo, and then stood with a dishcloth in her hands staring.

Honto's voice rose slowly, "Why did you take the picture? Did it ever dawn on you that the picture had more value than everything else you took? Insurance won't pay for a picture, it can't be replaced, and this child's photograph, so you know, is of their dead daughter who passed away just after it was taken. You stole the photo of a dead girl."

Guardia's eyebrow raised.

Honto continued, "Now I have a dilemma, which is to give the police back the photo which they surely desire with some of the jewelry, which costs us MONEY, M O N E Y, M O N E Y," he said slapping the table hard with his hands.

"Of course this means I have to admit some knowledge of what happened, which I don't want to do as that will again cost me MONEY, M O N E Y, M O N E Y, or...."

Pise pushed the door open, "I don't mean to interrupt, but if I have to cut his balls off tonight, I should do it now, because I'll have to clean up and it's late."

Guardia nodded "No," and closed the door with her hand.

At hearing of his balls being cut off and the look on Pise's face, and Alfardo's sure belief that Pise would in fact do that very thing, Alfardo peed his pants and it dripped from the wooden seat to the floor.

Alfardo was beside himself in ways he had never experienced; it was a terror which was physical. He remembered Pise's grip on his testicles and the intense pain. He stared at the table and did not look up.

"The picture had no value, why did you take it and why did you lie about it? Answer me now," yelled Honto.

"Let me talk with him alone," said Guardia. The door closed behind Honto as she sat alone with him.

"You took the photograph because a part of you is a child and you thought that photograph could be you in some better life. She's a pretty girl, that's true. But now the man in you must come forward because you put our family at risk by taking it…with no money in it for us, which is the worst thing you can do," said Guardia.

"Surely you understand that if this is found, it links us to the house. And if we don't get it back to the family, we have even worse trouble?"

Then she took his hand, "I will save your life tonight, but you will never do something like this, or anything else stupid like this again."

Honto walked back in the kitchen at that moment and brought in a large bag of jewelry, saying, "Pick two you took, make sure they came from that house."

Alfardo found two jeweled rings he knew were from the house and slid them toward Honto.

Honto took the framed photo and the rings, and a bottle of brandy, then turned to face Alfardo.

"I will try to undo your mess," he said as he left the house.

"Clean your mess," Guardia said pointing to the urine on the floor, and handing him two small towels, "then put your pants and the towels in this bag."

"You won't tell?," asked Alfardo.

"Tell what?," asked Guardia.

"That I peed myself," said Alfardo.

"Put the things in the bag and tie it shut at the top, and put it under the sink here," she said, leaving the room.

Alfardo removed his pants and used them to wipe up most of the urine on the floor and chair, then cleaned the floor and chair again with a towel, wet one end and put on soap, then scrubbed all, and got down on his hands and knees to sniff it and be sure there was no odor.

He washed himself off in front and on his buttocks with the other small towel, put all the items in the bag, tied it, placed it under the sink, and walked naked to his bedroom.

He closed the door and lay awake, haunted by dark and terrifying thoughts of what Pise would do to him with his knife.

SISTER GENA AND GIULIANA

Gena closed the door to Father Nicola's cottage, and walked quickly to the convent school.

She found Giuliana sitting on her bed staring out the window.

"Come with me, I need a little girl for something," said Sister Gena as she took Giuliana's hand and stroked her blonde curls.

"You have such beautiful hair, if I had ever had a daughter I would have wanted her to look just like you. The other children should be back soon, and you'll meet your roommate, I've arranged for you to be with Sara, she's a lovely girl and I know you will like her."

Giuliana was fascinated by Sister Gena; she was like a child, so short… she could look directly into Sister Gena's eyes, but was an adult.

Sister Gena went to a room and opened a dark wooden trunk and pulled out a soft sewn doll, all made of cloth with two black buttons for eyes.

"This little doll needs a mother to care for her, and I'm thinking you are just the one," said Sister Gena.

Giuliana took the doll and held it.

"I'm not sure if I'm lending it, or giving it, no, I'm giving it…so it's yours. And I have a secret…I made it!" said Sister Gena.

"She's pretty," said Giuliana as she clutched the doll.

Sister Gena kept the girl by her side and as they passed the front desk, known as *Sarna's Throne* to the children, Sarna said to Sister Gena, "A word please."

Giuliana was placed in the chair facing the desk, and the two nuns went to the kitchen. Soft whispers were heard, and then the two nuns reentered and Sister Gena took her hand again.

Sister Gena held her hand the entire time, and then about 3:00 in the afternoon a bus pulled into the drive and 30 children tumbled out, laughing and skipping.

VISITOR

The visitor did not leave her name, but merely presented herself to Sarna, saying she had a pressing matter to discuss with Father Nicola.

The visitor sat quickly at the table in the cottage, arranging her very plain dress, as distressed as any woman Father Nicola had ever seen.

"What I have to tell you, Father, I do not know if I should tell you, or not tell you. I find no peace either way."

He did not know her name so just sat silent, listening.

"Before you came, there was a priest who was sent away, and he was moved to another parish, far from here, and now I think he should be sent from there as well."

The story made no sense to Father Nicola. He simply raised his eyebrows, saying, "Go on."

"I see I make no sense to you so I'll tell you plainly. The priest touched little boys, he was caught here, and now he's doing it again in the town in which my sister lives."

She could tell from the look on the father's face that he was still in the dark.

"The priest engages in sexual behaviors, with little boys. Surely you've heard of this?"

Actually, Father Nicola had not heard of these things.

"What is the name of the priest?" he asked. She whispered the name in his ear.

Later that night, the father went to the home of a retired priest, Father Geno, a man who came from a farming background as Nicola had.

Father Geno said, "This is not a clear story…we have no proof, the family involved doesn't even go to this church any longer or even live in this town. I'll see what I can find, but I'm going to give you some good advice."

Father Nicola leaned forward, "There are things a young priest should concern himself with, and this is not one of them. You have your tasks, and it falls to others in the church to deal with such things. Personally, I have no firsthand knowledge of these happenings, but as I said, I'll look into it, but you should think about my advice."

Father Nicola walked back to the convent school slowly that evening, he thought about the words spoken to him, and spoken by him, and he felt an uneasiness in his stomach…and for the first time in his mission to serve Christ as a priest, he did not know what to do.

IN BED

Giuliana lay in bed unable to sleep. She looked at her roommate, Sara, and heard the girl's light breathing.

She liked the classes, and did well with teachers complimenting Giuliana on her work, and Sara was a sweet girl.

In hushed tones their first night together, Sara told Giuliana how her family had been running from the Germans, and planes came and the family got separated, but Sara was just a baby…and then a bomb hit the car with Sara's parents and they were blown apart so hard that there was nothing left of either.

Giuliana was so sorry to hear about Sara's experiences, it was so terrible.

Then Sara asked how it was that Giuliana was here, and so she told her.

"You mean your parents live so close? Why don't they take you home at night? Your parents are alive and you have to be here?" Sara asked.

Giuliana did not know the answers to those questions.

At meal times they sat at long tables and took turns serving the food.

Actually, at no time in her life had Giuliana felt so "watched." The nuns watched everything, and they were not unfair—in fact it was really hard to get into trouble even if you tried, other than that the nuns would talk to you forever about "your responsibilities," it was worse than a swat.

But the nights were hardest. Giuliana had so much trouble falling asleep. She'd get up to pee once or twice, but even that was watched, or heard, and if you didn't flush you might get caught for that and then have to listen to why it was important to flush; the explanations went on and on.

She tried to remember her father's trumpet, and could barely hear it in her mind. How was it memories of small things faded so quickly?

The bedroom door open just a slit, and little Sister Gena's eyes peered at Giuliana. Every night, sometimes twice, Sister Gena's little eyes would appear close to the doorknob level because the nun was so short, and then the door would close, and Giuliana could just barely hear the footsteps as she walked away.

STORE

It was Monday, and Silvia woke at 5 AM, leaving her husband Gennaro to sleep for a half hour longer.

She saw his trumpet on the floor, "What good are you, trumpet? You do no real work and have certainly made my life harder in many ways you don't know anything about."

She looked at Gennaro and thought how handsome he was and apologized to the trumpet, "I did not mean what I thought, you bring us beauty and my husband is a beautiful man." It was as her father had said: life with Gennaro would be like living with an exquisite painting from a museum, but day-to-day work would never be his strong suit.

"But what difference did it make; I do the work and do it better than him!," she thought as she laughed to herself.

She looked in the mirror as she wiped her face with the washcloth. *"Your face is strong, and people like you,"* her father had said, and, *"many a man has married a beauty to find she becomes less beautiful each day as he comes to learn of her selfishness and greed, and nasty tongue. But you, my Silvia, will always be more beautiful, because beauty is as beauty does."*

"Perhaps my eyes are beautiful," she thought, as she looked at their soft grey color with a hint of green.

She walked to the grocery and bought two cigarette lighters from her friend, who often sold her goods for her store when Silvia ran out.

"My order won't be here for two more days, thank you!" said Silvia. With the lighters in a bag, she walked to her own store and slipped the key into the lock, which was a smooth as butter, since its repair.

Silvia wore the store like a turtle wears a shell: it was a part of her, an extension of her, and her customers' little wants were known to her as well as her own wants.

Gaia stuck her head in the open door, "Are you open?"

"Always for you, come in, I'll be open in a half hour, but I'm glad to have the company."

"Oh Silvia, I need another four of the placemats with the picture of Giulianova, are there any left?," asked the woman who had known Silvia since their schooling as children.

"They're sold out but I'll go home at lunch and lend you mine, and then when the order comes in just give me mine back," said Silvia.

"Then let me pay you now, because I'll send my daughter for the placemats."

Silvia nodded and took the money. "What about Giuliana, do you miss her?" Gaia asked.

"How can I miss her, she's right over there. I have my hands full, and the nuns watch her like cats," said Silvia.

Gaia started to go, but turned, "Oh, I almost forgot, I hear that Splendora is thinking of leaving her children and going to America by herself."

"That's impossible," said Silvia. "Who will raise the children…who will feed her husband?"

"She doesn't care…imagine!" said Gaia as both began laughing.

"The price will be paid for many years," said Silvia.

SISTER GENA'S TEARS

Sister Gena knocked at the door of the cottage of the priest, Father Nicola.

"Come in, I'm always to glad to see you," he said, as he put his hand on the shoulder of the short and plump nun.

"I'm making jasmine tea, it's my one vice," he said, "Can I bring you some?"

She was quiet and he brought his mug of tea and pulled a chair near to Sister Gena's.

She began to cry, no sounds, just tears welling in her eyes, then dripping down her cheek.

As she made no move to remove them, he took a handkerchief out of his garment and wiped them.

"To what do we owe these tears?" he said.

"It's the girl Giuliana," said Sister Gena.

"She's in a wonderful place, she's cared for, and you watch her like a hawk…or more like a hen, and thank you for that," he said stroking her hand.

"She's so beautiful, and I would have liked to have a daughter like her," said Sister Gena.

"Ahhh," he said.

Silence.

"I grew up in a home of 7 sisters, and it was always assumed I'd become a nun," she said.

"You were always the one who cared for others, as you do here," he said.

"But I could have had another life—perhaps a marriage to a man, maybe a handsome man and musician like Giuliana's father, and a house that overlooks the sea, and children," said Sister Gena.

"Yes, there are always the paths not taken," said the priest. "For us all, even me. But keep in mind my dearest Sister Gena, that the only path we know is the one we took, the others are only our imaginings. Who knows how things would have turned out if you'd not become a nun."

"Is it a sin to love a girl like she is your daughter when she is not your daughter?" she asked.

"God cares for each of his children, so I think God is on your side on this one. There is a reason she is here, and maybe part of that reason is that Giuliana needs the kind of love a mother can give, and that you, while not her mother, do provide….a mother's love," he said as he lowered his head to look into her eyes.

"Yes?" she said.

"And so maybe we can be thankful to God that he has put her in our school, and thankful that it is a safe place for her and for us, and thankful that your love for her is a part of God's plan, and surely very pleasing for him, as I'm sure he saw that you have love in your heart to give to a child, and here the child is. I will pray to thank God for all this, perhaps you will do the same."

"Your words always make me feel better," she said.

He held Sister Gena's hand and she looked at her shoes, deep in thought, while he sipped his tea.

"I would like some tea too, exactly as you make it," she said smiling.

GYPSY FRUIT

Guardia placed a piece of fruit in Alfardo's hand and stroked his cheek as she walked back to the sink to prepare a meal.

Honto, the head of the Gypsy clan, came in with the greasy-haired young thief, Paulo, whose goatee now had grown to almost 6 inches beneath his chin.

Honto grabbed a pair of scissors from a drawer, and shoved Paulo into a chair at the table next to Alfardo, pointed the scissors at Paulo's eyes, then grabbed Paulo's goatee and cut it off.

"Next time I tell you to do something, do it," said Honto without anger.

"I thought you were kidding; I liked the way it looked, it's my…," said Paulo.

Honto reached to Paulo's cheek and grabbed it between two knuckles, hard, "I told you, you never do anything that can be noticed or remembered…this is smart business you'll find. Don't insult me by not listening to what I ask you again."

Alfardo was silent, watching someone else in trouble for once.

His goatee shorn, Paulo drove the truck, with Alfardo in the passenger seat.

"Shitty old man; I should have grabbed the scissors and put his eye out. He thinks he's smart and knows it all…he's a pig, he lives like a pig… are you listening to me?" Paulo said as he lit a cigarette.

"How long?," said Alfardo.

"What?," said Paulo.

"How long is this going to take?," said Alfardo.

"I don't know, we have to pick something up, but the bastard may not be there," Paulo said looking closely at the gypsy next to him.

"I'm trying to figure out if you're smart, or stupid," said Paulo.

"I heard about a guy who worked for a prick, like that horse's ass, Honto, but this guy was smart see, and found the prick's stash and robbed them—served 'em right," said Paulo.

"What you think of that?," said Paulo.

"I'm thinking that's a good way to end up dead," said Alfardo.

"That was just a test," said Paulo laughing, "I need to be sure you were loyal…loyalty is important."

A small dog was walking by the side of the road, and seeing it, Paulo swerved trying to clip it or run it over, but the dog saw him and jumped right and ran into a field.

"So you want to sleep with Alvana," said Paulo, "It's obvious."

"She is not interested in me," said Alfardo.

"Don't be too sure. For it to be good, you have to take a woman by force; it's how they want it; when they yell and scream and tell you to stop, it means you're turning them on and that they want it," said Paulo.

Alfardo was silent.

"Look," said Paulo, as he reached into his pocket and handed a new switchblade to Alfardo, opening it and poking Alfardo lightly in the side.

"Very nice, but you know we're not supposed to carry these, or guns, that's the rule," said Alfardo.

"I do what I want…it's for my personal use, not when I'm working," said Paulo.

"Where did you get it?" asked Alfardo.

"It was a gift."

Alfardo held it in his hand, "Well it has someone else's name inscribed on it," he said as he took a handkerchief and carefully wiped the blade and handle, then holding it by the handkerchief, he handed it back to Paulo.

"What, you think I wanted your fingerprints on it?" said Paulo, "that I was setting you up?"

"Just respect for your pretty new knife," said Alfardo as he looked out the window and tried to focus on the farms and animals they passed.

THE BEACH AT GIULIANOVA

Giuliana sat on the bus with the other children on the way to the beach at Giulianova, as Sabatina, Lea's husband, sat on the left of Giuliana, and Lea on Giuliana's right.

They held Giuliana's hands firmly in theirs, as the little nun, Sister Gena, turned back to look at them. Sister Gena turned around in her seat and climbed up onto her knees, peering over the back of her seat at them as a child might do with a large smile on her face.

"Your family misses you very much," said Lea, "and see, I have some candy from your mother from the store, and your father says to tell you he loves you." Lea kissed Giuliana's forehead, "but he has a performance this evening, and could not come."

"I'm trying to decide what to do, and you can help me," Sabatino said to Giuliana.

"My beautiful wife," and as he said this he looked at Lea's lovely brown eyes which he had found respite in so many times, "has said she wants a wooden rocking chair."

"But I've been looking into things, and there are dark-colored rocking chairs, and lighter-colored ones, which do you think she would prefer?"

"Oh, I love rocking chairs, and I like the dark ones with a little embroidered seat cushion best, and the cushion ties at the back so they don't fall off," said Giuliana as she looked at his salt and pepper colored hair, and his smile which seemed to fill his entire face.

"Can you believe it! This is exactly the chair I was thinking would be best, thank you my darling!" he said as he gave her a hug.

The bus swayed left and right as they followed the back roads that flowed with the undulating hills, and here and there, the Adriatic Sea could be seen in the distance, behind the olive groves and grape vines as they passed farm after farm.

Then a very steep winding section of road took them into Giulianova, which had many shoppes with visitors from all over Italy, Switzerland, Germany and the Baltic countries.

"See you back at the bus in three hours," said Sister Gena as she stroked Giuliana's hair and stuck a chocolate covered almond in the girl's mouth, "take care of my little chicken," she said to Lea and Sabatino as the nun turned to herd the other children, telling them where to stand and what to bring and what to leave on the bus.

There were wooden benches in groupings where people could sit and look at the sea…so calm today it resembled a lake, with the coastline a gentle crescent curvature left to right. Out in the distance was a sailing boat with two sails moving slowly. The sails would luff, then fill with wind; just barely enough to keep the boat moving.

Lea had shopping to do, so Sabatino took Giuliana's hand and they walked through the cabanas and chairs and lounges on the beach, onto on a concrete walkway, and removed their shoes to walk in the sea.

"And so, I hear you are well-liked and doing well?" he said.

"Yes," said Giuliana.

"I think Sister Gena cares for you very much," he said.

Giuliana nodded, "Can I ask you something?" she said.

"Yes, anything," he answered.

"If you had a little girl, would you send her away?"

He stopped and walked up onto the dry sand, 20 feet from the water, sitting with her.

"One of the great secrets in life, and I'll share this with you like my Grandmother told it to me, and the way I remember it always…look for the good in all that happens," he said.

"What does that mean?" Giuliana said as she looked down at the sand.

"Well, your family is close by, you know they are safe, and they know you are safe, and not everyone in life is safe…"

"Who's not safe?" she asked.

"Well in times of war, people are missing, and some never return."

"Are we in a war?"

"No, no, I'm not saying we are in a war. I know your being separated from your family is very difficult for you, but you are getting the best education in the world, in a school which offers you safety."

"It's not what I want," said Giuliana.

"You are very wise, yes, it is not what you want, but it's what you have, and the smart move is to look for the good. Why don't you think about it. You decide."

"Why are you so nice to Lea?," asked Giuliana.

"Ohhh, well, you see couples are of two types: one thinks that arguing is the road to happiness, but another way to love is more gentle and more kind…and she and I are like that."

"Do you buy her things?"

"I'm a bus driver, and I don't have a large amount of money, but I tell her I love her every day…because I do love her every day, and I bring her little things. You know, things mean much less than people think, but even something small can mean a lot. But everybody knows when they are loved."

A pained looked came to his face, as if he'd crossed a boundary he did not care to approach, and he jumped up saying, "Well let's keep walking and find some shells for Lea," and the two walked along the water with the Adriatic Sea at their toes, and sifted through the sand with their fingers until they found two small shells which were perfect with no flaws.

DINNER

There were 30 girls in the school, because one had left to live with a family in Switzerland, and Giuliana and one other girl were the only two who were not orphans.

Some parents had died, such as Giuliana's roommate Sara's, some had abandoned their children, and for some, the nuns apparently didn't know what happened to their parents.

The two girls were close friends now, and Giuliana liked to squeeze Sara's hair which had a much tighter kinky curl than the others, and loved her deep olive skin and long slender fingers and the shape of the fingernails; so long and graceful.

Some of the children accused Sara of being black, but the nuns said no she was not black, and to stop gossiping about others.

"I'm sick and tired of explaining why I'm in this school," said Giuliana as they ate alone at a small table.

"What do you mean?" asked Sara.

"How did your parents die? I hear it over and over until I want to slap them," said Giuliana.

"That's just because their parents are all dead; everybody here has a story, they just want to know about you," said Sara.

Giuliana thought about telling Sara this next part, but was silent.

"What?," said Sara, who poked Giuliana's head saying, "When you stop talking I know you start thinking, so….what is it?"

Giuliana spoke slowly, "As soon as I explain that my parents are alive, they want to know where they are, and then when I tell them they live just 5 minutes away…"

Giuliana stopped talking and Sara just looked at her fork as she ate her meal.

HOME

On Sundays, all the children from the convent school went to church as a group in Mosciano, walking and giggling and skipping, and dropped Giuliana off at her home at 3:00.

Giuliana stayed at home for just 3 hours, with the students coming to get her at 6, when church was over.

Giuliana knocked at her front door, and it felt so strange; to knock on a door which was her own home; where she used to go in and out every day whenever she wanted.

Her father, Gennaro came to the door and gave her a hug and a kiss.

She sat in the kitchen as her mother prepared a meal, but her mother's eyes did not look at her, and then Giuliana went up to her bedroom.

Giuliana's room had changed; the furniture had been moved, the bed was nearer the wall, and there was a new photo on the table.

She went to the window and saw the sparkling light blue of the Adriatic Sea far in the distance, then ran to the other side of the room to see the grays and light terra cotta colors of the Gran Sassos mountains.

She was afraid; afraid the day would pass too quickly, and all she could think about was that she didn't want to go back to the school, but to stay here at home and watch her mother and hear her father's playing of his trumpet.

But she knew that no matter what she said, she was going back to the school, and so she sat on the bed and stared at the wall.

David E. Kettlewell

LEA AND SABATINA IN EVENING

Lea's husband, Sabatino, had taken a bath, brushed his teeth with baking soda and carefully gargled until no trace of the taste was left in his mouth, clipped his nose hairs and trimmed his eyebrows and looked in the mirror.

"Not bad for a salt and pepper," he said seeing the gray and white hairs encroaching on his coarse dark hair.

He turned off the light and walked to the bedroom, removed his slippers and robe and placed his body next to his wife Lea.

He stroked her hair, "What's bothering you?"

"She breaks my heart. What I feel is beyond my words to express," Lea said.

Sabatino said in her ear, "But my love, you adore her and she knows that, you do all you can, and what you do is a lot."

Lea answered, "Giuliana knows, I know she knows."

"Knows what?" he asked.

"That they're not there for her; that her mother doesn't really care. Children know so much, only they can't say it," Lea said.

"Then she knows you love her. But everyone has a different way of showing love," he said. "Silvia has a shoppe to run, and you and I know nothing of her personal burdens so we should not judge, and I know for a fact that Gennaro adores his daughter."

"What is he, what kind of man would do this, would go along with this?" she asked.

"Well that one I know the answer to…someone married to Silvia, because she is a Grilli, and there is only one way for a Grilli…their own way, now this I know you know," he said.

Sabatino added, "But there is something else; she's just a little girl, and do you remember when your father would say to look at the bright side of things? You tell this to people all the time. There is some good in Silvia, just think about it."

"You'd say these things to me even if they weren't true, just to comfort me," Lea said.

Lea pressed her lips to his and they held each other listening to the light wind in the night, and she was his again.

GYPSIES… ALFARDO IN BED

Alfardo was staying at the gypsy house for two days and two nights; it was a rare treat.

He lay in bed thinking of Alvana; of her smooth tan skin with a hint of olive, and her long dark hair and dark eyes which came alive in brown hues in the sun.

Of her soft, sensually-shaped lips, and her innocence.

She moved quietly throughout the house when he was there, which was not often.

He remembered the day he opened the bathroom door and she turned to reveal her breasts to him, pouring water over her body and staring into his eyes.

So brazen.

"I could take her to another place, and she would fall deeply in love with me and make love to me every night."

He thought about the quickness of the whores he'd been with, and how he'd want it slower with Alvana, and wanted her to kiss him gently, and rock gently.

And he thought about stroking her and touching her, and the taste of her kiss on his tongue, and her saying, "It's alright, I want to have your baby. It's alright."

And he put on one of his socks and lay on his pillow as if it were her, and kissed her passionately in his dreams, and more, then dressed and took his two socks into the bathroom and washed them both, and hung them to dry over his closet door and fell to sleep with thoughts of her arms holding him and her gentle kisses on his cheeks.

Vittoria's Diary

GYPSIES... PAULO'S FOUL MIND

Paulo drove the truck to her house and thought about what he would do. She'd looked at him and he knew she wanted it.

She would struggle, and maybe cry and beg, but he knew what she wanted….he would tear her clothes off, and slap her across her face and tie her hands behind her back.

He'd take her every way he could and take pleasure in the light blows with his fists to her abdomen.

Then he might untie her hands, then tie her to the bed and take her screaming.

And after he would watch her weep or shake, and he would smoke a cigarette and laugh at her antics, and maybe flick the cigarette ash at her.

"Sex is control, and women want a man to control them, and the rougher the better," the thief from Rome had said.

"Never take no for an answer, make them do as you say. Show them you are a man," the thief added.

It especially brought him pleasure to see a woman weep after he'd taken them.

Down deep, he knew; he knew women were all whores, even the porcelain ladies, the rich ones who hoddy-toddied all their lives, soaked in luxury.

He understood what women wanted, and gave it to them.

And he thought how lucky he was to be young and strong, and how he could take what he wanted from life…and of his power.

That night, he prepared the heroin—and this was good stuff with a kick- in the silver spoon he'd stolen, and took out the syringe with the glass plunger and needle, filled it, tied off his arm and shot the drug into his veins, watching his arm as he released the tie and fell into a stupor, seeing the house he'd live in with all the things he'd taken from fools.

"I could run the family," he blurted before he passed out.

GYPSY EYES

Guardia entered the room Alfardo had slept in and peered at everything closely. She saw the socks drying on the closet door and sniffed the bed.

Walking into the kitchen she said, "Alfardo has been doing a good job?"

Honto's eyes rose from his record book to look at her. He nodded, "yes".

"He needs a woman," Guardia said.

"All men need a woman, all real men. What business is that of ours?" said Honto.

"Maybe Alfardo should move in with us here," she said.

Honto said nothing, but just stared at his book intently.

"What more?" he asked.

"He has an interest in Alvana, I can see it in his eyes," she said.

"You mean you can see it in his pants," he said as a small smile broke his stone face.

"He makes us money," she said.

"Yes, he makes us money, and that is why he cannot live here, because the type of work he does has risks, and I don't want him living here because of that," Honto said.

"You have friends to get him out of trouble if he gets caught," she said.

"That depends on who catches him," Honto said. "Come sit."

She sat next to him and put his hand on her knee.

"So you're a matchmaker, are you?" he said.

"Why not, she has to go to somebody, there are many who are worse," she said.

"I have somebody else in mind for her," he said.

"You mean you have the dream of somebody better for her," she said.

She continued, "Then put him in another line of work and let him live here, and we'll see what happens between them."

He nodded, "No".

She scratched his knee.

"I know what will happen if he lives here; what's in his pocket will be inside of her, is this supposed to surprise anyone?" said Honto.

"Think about them, it could work," she said.

"You've developed a soft spot for him, maybe he's too soft," said Honto.

"I don't tell you how to do your business," she said abruptly but respectfully.

"I will think about it…see, you've won," said Honto.

"Another thing," said Guardia, "I don't want that Paulo in this house again."

He looked into her eyes for some time. "What did he do to you?"

"I heard he was rough with a woman, very rough," she said.

"You mean he was rough with a whore, and how is that our concern?" then he added, "I have plans for Paulo, he's a man."

"He doesn't come in the house again," she said slapping the table with a dishrag. "Let him be a man somewhere else."

"I don't tell you how to run your house," Honto said gently.

Then Honto put the book down, "I'll see about the woman whose nose he bloodied…you see I am not so stupid as you think," he said as Guardia came around to rub his shoulders, while she kissed the top of his graying head and ran her hand down his back.

"And I'll think about this poor little thief Alfardo for Alvana, so he doesn't wear out his socks," he said as they both broke into laughter so loud it could easily be heard outside.

David E. Kettlewell

LIGHT TAN SHOES

Gennaro pulled the thin cream-colored wool socks with the little grey diamond decorative pattern over his feet, then pulled up his pressed trousers, sliding the alligator belt through the pant loops.

A fresh white shirt was taken from the drawer; his favorite as the cloth was so finely woven and smooth to the skin, with a straight collar—no buttons, and slid it over his arms and torso, then carefully put on the cufflinks.

He tucked the shirt in carefully and stepped back to look in the mirror.

"Not a bad look at all," he said as he positioned the collar with his hands and sat on the bed, sliding his feet into the light tan shoes with the decorative leather cover piece which went over the laces.

He'd taken 2 months to make these shoes, and they were based on a picture he'd seen in a men's magazine.

He remembered the smell of his father's cobbler shoppe and the deep whirring of the motors which spun the polisher, and his father who worked at shoe making with a depth of focus seen in all true craftsman.

"This will give you a living your entire life, not poverty like a musician's life," his father had said one day, aware his son had a gift with music, but clear it never paid all the bills on time.

Gennaro, age 9, did not answer him, but applied more polish to the shoes he worked on.

"The man that makes and repairs quality shoes has the life of a rich man: he has food, a roof over his head, and savings," his father added.

Gennaro stood and looked again in the mirror. He had what Chopin had called *Bon Tot*…the exquisite dress of a man that said success—and he'd done it his way with music, as he told everyone he'd do.

"These shoes are just a bit tight," thought Gennaro as he walked to the

Piazza enjoying the bright morning sunshine and pure air in the perfect 72 degree weather of the paradise of Mosciano Sant'Angelo, "they'll loosen in time, leather always does."

Every woman who saw him smiled or touched his elbow. "Look at you, so handsome, it's too bad you're not single…and me too!" they would think, and then smile.

And the men always stopped, nodding to him and speaking of his music.

"Gennaro, do you think I can learn to play trumpet like you? I heard you play last week…what a gift you have, what a tone! You should travel to America and play Carnegie Hall," one said.

Bertonio sat at the café and waved to Gennaro. He walked over and sat down, being careful not to crinkle the back of his suit coat.

"A cappuccino," Gennaro said to the waitress who brought it to him but said she would take no money. "Your trumpet is the voice of God," she said knowing her mother would be pleased.

Gennaro began, "Of course, you know Silvia; everything she does, she does well, but Silvia and I do not see eye-to-eye on Giuliana."

"So it will be her way," said Bertonio laughing.

"I sometimes wish she would listen to me more, or even pretend she's listening. I don't think she even hears my words. The truth is, and don't ever share this and I tell only you…I feel ashamed for what was done to Giuliana. She should be home with us," Gennaro said.

"There would be no 'us' you speak of now if Giuliana were home, because Silvia is a rock, and you wouldn't have a marriage," said Bertonio.

"I can make it up to Giuliana," said Gennaro.

"Yes," said Bertonio smiling, "I'm sure you will."

How strange, thought Bertonio, to have the talent to play music like a God, but a household not his own.

But he said nothing, as being a true friend is often about what you don't say more than what you do.

Bertonio brought his cappuccino to his lips and savored the flavors on his tongue and palate; the dancing interplay he loved of the sweetness and the bitter.

2 years later

VITTORIA'S DIARY

It was 4 in the afternoon. Giuliana took the homework she'd worked on and crumpled it into a little ball, then went outside to throw it down the ravine where it landed with 6 other crumpled balls of paper she'd thrown there earlier in the week.

She knew this would mean she would have to help with dishes again tonight, but she was on a mission.

Her bed was not made, nor had she made it for a week.

Actually, she'd done everything wrong she could think of, from talking in class to refusing to answer the nuns who taught her.

The catholic convent school teaching staff, all nuns, reacted gently as they'd seen this happen so many times over the years with others, and they knew Giuliana was a good girl.

On Sunday, Giuliana's mother sent her to her room for one hour, saying, "So you think that if you misbehave, you won't have to stay at the school? Well it won't work with me."

"You're a little conniving little thing, but we'll fix that," her mother said, "and stop sticking your tongue out and biting it with your teeth, or I'll put soap on it."

This was a peculiar habit Giuliana had developed over the last few months; it seemed to bring her comfort for reasons she did not understand.

Giuliana stood at her window looking at the Adriatic Sea, and thought of her diary and what she would write.

She lay on the bed thinking.

She opened the diary given to her by Lea, she'd dreamed of so, which was massive; over one foot high and almost as wide, with a carved dark wooden cover having a rectangular casting of Jesus on the Cross set into the wood in the center. The pages were light cream with gold on the edges. It was the most beautiful diary in the world.

She opened it and wrote on the first page, "Vittoria's Diary."

It seemed so thin and alone, those words.

"I should have written bigger," she said.

Then she turned the page and wrote, "My parents are unfair; my mother is mean to me and my father doesn't care that I hate living at the convent school. They make me go to a school for orphans, and the other kids think there is something wrong with me, I know they do."

Then she grew afraid she would be caught and hid the diary, and lay on the bed pretending to nap, thinking of lions in Africa she'd read about in class.

Vittoria's Diary

WORDS

Gennaro entered the small meat shoppe in the Piazza by the far side door and was looking at postcards of Rome on a rotating wire display, when he heard two women on the opposite side of the store talking. He could just see them as he peered through the rack of cards.

"The poor girl is stuck living in that convent school and that monster acts like the girl is not even alive. I've seen her do some hard things, but this goes beyond that," said the first whose voice Gennaro did not recognize.

"He's a wonderful man, and a darling, why does he put up with it?" said the second.

"The only thing I can figure is that the little girl is not his daughter. She's a love child, that would explain that wench dumping her in the convent school," said the first.

"That's impossible! Who would take Silvia? She's as plain as a barn door," said the second, as they both began laughing.

"Hush, she's coming," said the first as the store proprietor appeared from the back.

"Something else for you?" said the owner.

"No, we were just looking," answered one of the women as they exited the store together and turned left on the sidewalk, towards the bread store.

Gennaro stayed hidden until he was sure they were gone, then walked out quickly, heading straight home.

Neighbors of Gennaro and Silvia remembered this as the only evening when they could hear Gennaro's voice over his wife's typically higher pitched tirades.

Within weeks, Gennaro and Silvia decided to bring Giuliana home when she turned 7 to enter 3rd grade.

HOME

At 7 years old, and after 3 years living apart from her family, Giuliana was to be set free… returned to her family.

Unclear as to why she'd been sent to the convent school in the first place, and unclear why she'd been freed, she sat looking at the small backpack of things she would take with her. A box on the floor in her bedroom at the convent school held the things she could not carry in the backpack.

Her roommate Sara was gone from the school with the other girls, as was her friend Gena, and she stepped outside the front door.

She was afraid that she was dreaming, and would wake up and be back at the school. She closed the door and jumped down the steps.

Father Nicola was watching from some distance, he walked towards her.

"You didn't think we'd let you walk home alone?" he said.

He took her hand and they walked.

"I would imagine you have a lot of feelings right now. I know the school was many things, but it was not home. You may find a happiness at home now which you did not feel before, that's my hope," the priest said.

She said nothing but just walked along, imagining what living at home would be like; how she would hear her father's trumpet again.

She did not glance at the Adriatic Sea or the mountains, or the shoppes, or the Piazza, or the gelato store which had opened, but just stared straight ahead in the direction of home.

"Goodbye," she said to the priest almost absent-mindedly, as she jumped up on the stoop and opened the door to home.

GIULIANA'S BROTHER CLAUDIO

Two years after returning home, when Giuliana was 8 ½ years old, Giuliana's mother had a baby boy named Claudio.

For the first few months when nursing, Gennaro looked after the shoppe in the mornings, while Silvia stayed home with the baby.

Then, switching roles, Gennaro would care for the baby while Silvia worked the store, but care of the child was entrusted to Giuliana from the time she returned from school each day.

Silvia gave Giuliana a long list of what she was to do and not to do, how she was to handle an emergency, and how to feed Claudio.

Giuliana was nervous about her new assignment, but excited.

She loved to stroke his hair, and give him a bath, and dry him while he laughed and she would grab his nose playfully, but was horrified one day.

Claudio ate everything in front of him, developed a light fever, and fell into a short epileptic fit.

"This will pass as the child ages…he does not have epilepsy," Dr. Rinaldo had promised the parents, but it sent chills through Giuliana's body every time his fits began.

Nothing she could do would help, she simply had to wait until he stopped.

As the child grew, he came to view Giuliana as his mother, and his eyes would follow her like a cat. If she spoke he would obey, and when scared, he called for her.

His first words were "Sachio," the pet name he had for Giuliana. She was so proud of those words. She would sit and hold his fingers and raise and lower his arms, and they'd say Sachio over and over, with Giuliana laughing and kissing his cheeks.

"I think you have stolen this child," said Silvia, adding, "the truth is you are doing a very good job for such a little girl."

Giuliana was so shocked when she heard these soft words from her mother, she could not remember a time in her entire life when she'd heard anything other than biting criticism from her mother.

Gennaro heard it also and lowered his newspaper to see his daughter's smile, then lifted it again before she could see his eyes.

Two years later...

A CONVERSATION WITH THE PRIEST

Father Nicola now had a very small home in Mosciano Sant'Angelo, just a bit down the road from the convent school, but he still had an office in the cottage next to the school, as people had become familiar with visiting him there.

The knock at the door was soft.

"Olympia, come in," he said.

A beautiful young woman of 22, with rich black hair which hung straight down on both sides of her oval face appeared. She was not Greek, but Italian, as much of Italy had been under the military rule of Greece in ancient times. The Greeks were gone, but the names remained.

"She has the classic beauty of a model for Michelangelo: those oval eyes, and exquisitely-fashioned lips," thought Father Nicola.

"So, you wanted to talk with me," he said making tea with a smile, as like all men, he loved the company of beautiful women.

"Yes," she answered. "I don't know that you'll know what I'm saying, priests don't....," and she stopped.

He raised his eyebrows and sat, waiting for the water pot to whistle.

She continued, "It's men. In the beginning, you know, when I first start seeing a man, I have this idea in my mind of how I want to be treated, and how things can be, and I feel something, something like love but maybe more just a dream of love…but then by the time I deal with all the problems of getting to know them, and I'm actually in a place where I could love them…I find I don't love them at all anymore. I'm so disappointed in how they've behaved. Do you think that's normal?"

"Why do you find them objectionable?" the priest asked.

"They're rude, selfish, they don't consider my feelings, and expect me to do everything their way, and they all want sex, which they're not going to get…from me," she said.

"What do your parents do, again?" he asked.

"My father is a lawyer, and my mother has a medical practice in Rome. They don't live together," said Olympia.

"Well, you're obviously intelligent, from a family of intelligent parents…but also from a family with challenges regarding love, which we all have. In my experience…or better put; years of listening experience," he said with a smile, "I think there are two truths at play with love: one is the mind, and the other the heart. Trying to get the two to work together seems a challenge for just about everyone I know."

"What do you think I should do?," she asked.

"Some movement towards a more forgiving approach to men's actions, and finding a man who is a better fit could be an answer."

As he walked to the Piazza after the meeting he thought about relationships.

"People struggle as if gasping for air to find love and marriage, then when they are in the marriage all they can think about is how to change it, or get out. I wonder why that is?"

He saw Giuliana from a block away. She ran out of her mother's store and jumped on a green bicycle and began riding toward him.

She stopped, straddling the bicycle.

"Father, it's good to see you. How is everyone at the convent?"

He looked at her and could scarcely believe it. She was stunningly beautiful at only 13, with a fully mature woman's body, the breasts of a woman, shapely legs, and a fire in her eyes reflecting the singular energy of youth.

"They miss you," the priest said, "Sister Gena says if you don't come to see her more often she will bite you," at which Giuliana laughed.

"How is your brother, Claudio?" the priest asked.

"I help take care of him. Visitors think he's my son, isn't that funny?" said Giuliana. "Are you headed to see my mother?"

"No, I just like to walk in the mornings and say hello to the people."

"Well I'm glad you said hello to me, bye," she said as she put her foot on the pedal. "I have to take it back soon, so I have to go," she said as she rode off waving at him. He watched as the wind caught her hair and her legs pumped furiously, as if she had but one ride in life and this was it… to be savored like fine food or wine.

The priest saw Giuliana's mother's store up ahead, but did not stop, instead going into the fruit store. He looked at each wooden crate stacked upon others, looking at the beautiful colors of the oranges and grapes and mangoes.

"Father, take what you want," said Nera.

She worked and arranged her displays: the long units along the wall holding apples, oranges, and figs, then the stacked crates, one upon another made of dry coarse wood held together with nails, the crate on top open to show the luscious fruit at just the right height to reach out and touch.

"Oh no, I just look," he answered, as he stood with his head bent forward. He lifted one mango and sniffed its end, seeing a bit of sap.

"They're ripe," said Nera.

"Yes, I see," he answered.

BIAGIO'S JOURNEY

"I'm studious and conservative and a hard worker and come from a good family and I love her so completely I can't say hardly, and I love her," thought Biagio as he looked at the piece of writing paper in front of him, pen in hand.

He was not satisfied with his appearance.

"I'm too plain, nothing stands out." He went to the mirror and looked at himself. He was average in height, average in weight, and non-descript.

"I have nice hair, it's thick and curly. She might like that," he thought as he ran his hand though it.

She was perfect. "My god, that figure, it comes out and hits you on your eyeballs, and that spunky body and fun laugh, and lips, I'm going to kiss those lips, and I'm going to tell her I love her, ask her to marry me, and she'll say yes and I'll make love to her all night the evening of our wedding. It's not wrong if you're married."

He went back to the paper in front of him.

He wrote a long letter, but felt it was too scholarly, then crumpled it up and threw it in the little trash can that looked like the Tower of Pisa. Then he wrote another version and threw it in the trash, then another, and another.

"Just tell her the important stuff, maybe, maybe she'll love me too," he thought.

When done, he folded the note, and it began its convoluted journey to Giuliana.

Later that day, Biagio's mother opened each balled-up letter in the trash can and read every word.

GIULIANA'S FIGURE

Giuliana sat reading a book in the little shoppe while her mother served the customers.

There was a lull, so Silvia eyed her daughter. Those bulging breasts infuriated her, her daughter's figure was so…full.

"Giuliana, go home and change. I can see your breasts, it's disgusting…and I told you…stop sucking and biting on your tongue."

Such a peculiar habit: she would stick her tongue out and bite gently on it.

Giuliana looked down at her white top; her breasts were not showing at all.

"They're not showing," said Giuliana. "…the blouse has a curved front, nothing is showing, and you're looking down."

"Stop flaunting your body, go home and cover up those breasts now," her mother yelled.

Giuliana knew that discussions with her mother were a total waste of time, her mother wouldn't listen to a freight train if were bearing down on her.

She gently put her book down, "Alright," she said and walked to her home.

A friend of Silvia's came into the shoppe.

"Those young boys, Silvia, they're coming in the store just to stare at her, did you put her in the store to draw young men's business?"

Silvia exploded.

"What? Of course not. That figure of Giuliana's…every man out there is going to want to take advantage of her, they look at her all the time, she's going to get pregnant. That Biagio is a curse, he's too old for her, far too old, and goes to school in Teramo. Why does he want a girl that young? I know what he wants…and he'll get it, you'll see," said Silvia nastily.

"Calm down Silvia, she's a good girl, she's not having sex. She can't help that she's beautiful."

And Giuliana was certainly beautiful, as she walked home every man included in the "birds on a wire," saw her and followed each step she made…the liveliness, the sway of her body, her legs and the beautiful figure, brown eyes and dark shoulder-length hair.

"My God, it's a body to match Sophia Loren," one said.

"Better," said another.

"Much better," intoned another.

She was the prettiest girl in town, with no pretentions, and she was Gennaro's daughter, and he was wonderful.

Giuliana walked to the little stone bench for two at the end of the Piazza, and took the letter out of her pocket given to her by Biagio.

My Dearest Giuliana,

I love you. I don't know that you know what I mean by this, because I'm so much older.

But I love you.

I see you walk and talk, and I think, no, I know, you are the girl I want to marry.

Please believe in our love, because we can make it happen.

I'm going to be a professor, and we can get married and have children.

You are so beautiful you are the only thing I see in my life.

I think about you and my kiss is on your cheek!

Think about my love for you, and ask if you love me too?

Your Love,

Biagio

A month prior when she'd first been handed the letter by a girlfriend, she went to Lea's home.

Giuliana was only 13 years old and really didn't have any interest in men at all, nor did she know anything about sex or what led up to it.

Lea read the letter.

"I don't understand, why did he write to me?" said Giuliana laughing and bumping into Lea's shoulders playfully on the couch.

"He's saying he loves you," said Lea.

"What do you mean? He's not my family," said Giuliana.

Lea looked at Giuliana, and saw that she was no longer a little neighbor girl, but a beautiful young woman. Somehow she had not really seen it before.

"Well, you certainly know that men look for a woman to love and to have children with, and he's telling you he loves you and wants you to think about whether you love him."

"I'm only 13, what does he want?" asked Giuliana.

"I think he wants to be friends," said Lea.

Giuliana put away the letter and walked the few blocks to home, heard her father practicing and went in and kissed his forehead, and went up to her room.

She looked at her figure in the mirror.

She put a light blue pullover sweater on which went up to her neck.

"Maybe this will satisfy her," she said and ran back to the store.

The "birds on a wire" watched her as she ran, savoring the gentle bouncing up and down of her beautiful figure, and more than one had his mouth open in a gaping pose.

WASHING CLOTHES

Giuliana carried the cold water in buckets from the kitchen to the cement washing tub at the front of the yard, with its two large rollers and crank she'd use to extract the water from the clothes after washing them. Cold running water had been added to the home when she was 10.

She was lucky; today was a small wash with only three shirts, two pairs of pants, four pairs of stocks, some stockings, three towels, and no sheets because they were washed in the fountain in town.

She placed all the laundry in the tub and poked the clothing into the cold water. The tin tank by the stove in the kitchen provided some hot water for cleaning dishes and baths, but was not used for clothes. She did not know why, "Maybe the tank is too small."

She slipped the bar of soap into the water and rubbed some into the first shirt, working it over and over on the corrugated galvanized ramp with the ribbles, up and down and up and down and then flipped it to work the other side.

Then she dunked the shirt into the water again and placed it into the bowl she'd put on the grass for rinsing later. After rinsing, the clothes would be cranked through the rollers and hung on the string secured with the smoothly carved wooden clothes pins.

It was confusing to her.

A month ago she'd received a love letter from Biagio, a man who said he loved her. Now, today she'd received a package from an aunt in America; a very delicate small tea set with gold ornamentation and a child's doll.

She laughed.

"Am I a woman or am I a child? Which is it? What am I going to do with a doll? Maybe I can give it to a child."

But she thought she'd keep the tea set as she'd put it on the shelf in her bedroom along with the china horse and the little glass clown.

She knew she was no longer a little girl, but instead was now a woman with a new boyfriend much older than she—a young woman who had essentially raised her mother's child, Claudio.

She was not reluctant in the least to let go of the dream of childhood as her childhood years had been anything but easy, and her time at the convent school a kind of prison really, although she'd been treated with kindness by all there.

"Why did they send me in the first place?" she thought, and anger bit at her as it always did when she thought of being banished from her home against her will.

It did not escape her mind that her mother's plans for her at home were to care for Claudio, but she adored him really above all else in ways she would have difficulty describing. He was not her child, but he was, and the bond between the two was like the grains in wood…intermingled forever.

She remembered the time he had choked on a large gnocchi, and she poked her fingers into his throat to pull it out, and how he'd clung to her afterwards.

"Maybe I'll give away the tea set as well as the doll," she thought. "It's too small, really."

SILVIA'S EDICT

Silvia sat at her kitchen table with Biagio, alone.

"I understand you like Giuliana," she said coldly.

He nodded, "I love your daughter and want to marry her."

"Then I don't want you to see her and talk with her away from our home. If you want to see her you come to the house and sit with the family. That's the only way you can see her, and if you don't do this, you won't see her at all," Silvia said.

"No, no, this is wonderful," said Biagio, "I can come and study with her and get to know your family, because we'll all be family when she and I are married," and he leaned forward to give her a kiss on her cheek, but she held up her hand.

As he walked home he thought, "This is wonderful, I get to see her, I can't believe it," and he went to his mother to share his good fortune.

IN THE STORE

"Because if I don't allow him in the house, she'll see him behind my back, I know she will. He follows her around the town, always talking to her. I need to keep an eye on both of them," said Silvia.

"But what about the other boys in town? They all come in here wanting to see her, but she's already got a boyfriend, and she's only 13. They get no chance at all," said the woman whose nephew wanted to date Giuliana.

Silvia said nothing.

LOVE & BIAGIO'S MOTHER

Biagio's mother tied the apron behind her back, and sliced the apples carefully with the paring knife, taking off just the thinnest skin.

"I love your fresh apple pie," said Biagio, who was studying at the kitchen table while his mother cooked.

She sliced off a piece of apple and threw it at him which he caught easily with his hand, quickly put it in his mouth, chewing loudly.

"Try that again," he said laughing, "I'll eat the next one too!"

"So, my budding young man, do you have any girlfriends at school?" his mother asked.

The conversation between the two was easy and close. It had always been that way.

"You are very thorough in your cleaning," he said.

"You wouldn't have left the crumpled notes in the trash can if you hadn't wanted me to see them…I know you," she said as she sat with him, placing the fleshy apple pieces into one smaller white bowl and the discards in another.

His hand dipped into the smaller bowl and grabbed a piece quickly and popped it into his mouth.

"How am I going to keep up with you?" she said.

"I can go get more apples, it won't take me long," he offered.

"No, I have more. You keep reading your books," she said.

"She's the girl I want to marry," he said staring at the pages, not looking into her eyes.

"Don't you think she's a little young for you? She's only 13. There are things you want maybe she doesn't want," said his mother.

"I'm only 4 years older and it seems like a lot now, but it won't be when we're older. Father is 6 years older than you," he replied.

"Yes, but we met in our twenties. I know she's a beautiful girl, but you have no idea who she will be when she is older, when she matures," she said.

"Do you really know her? Who she is inside?" she asked her son.

"I think so, yes," he said.

"Has she seen your letter?" asked his mother.

"Yes."

"How did you get it to her?," his mother asked.

"The first through a friend of ours, but now her little brother, Claudio is our messenger. He does exactly what she tells him. If she sends me a note, he won't leave me until I write one for her, right then!"

"Really," he continued, "he says he's not allowed to go back without a note from me…it's like he's in her army, or works for her," he said.

"Well, I know how you feel about her. I'm glad for you, she's your first love…if she likes you back. I think she will because you're charming and handsome, like a prince," the mother said.

"She likes me back," he said, lifting his eyes to hers.

She saw a soft milkiness in his eyes; a look of a very young man infatuated in love.

"But I want you to think about something, my love, and you should think deeply," said his mother.

"What?"

"When you marry someone, you marry their family," she said.

"He's a gentleman and marvelous musician, everyone likes him," Biagio said.

"I wasn't thinking of him, everyone loves Gennaro," she answered.

"Her mother, Silvia?" said Biagio, "She works hard. She doesn't have an education, but most people don't from her time."

"From her time?" said his mother with a laugh.

"You know what I mean," he said.

His mother added, "She also cheats at cards, and pushes people around, and she doesn't listen, and her head and her heart are closed. She's a Grilli," said his mother.

"What does, 'She's a Grilli,' mean? I've heard others say it," he asked.

"Her family name is Grilli…the family is filled with people with strong opinions who are hard-headed; a kind of hard-headed you've never seen. Her father and grandfather were worse, you really couldn't reason with any of them."

"Giuliana's not like that," he said.

"I'm not talking about Giuliana, and I'm not talking about Gennaro, I'm talking about her, about Silvia," his mother said.

"I thought you liked her," he said.

"I like her because she helped me once, and lent me money to tide us over. But I know what she's like, and you don't know what she might do."

She could tell that her words were not really understood, as he did not respond.

She placed her hand on his arm. "Love is always a risk. Of course the most important thing is if Giuliana decides she loves you. If she's smart, she'll grab you up like that," she said snapping her fingers, as she stroked her hands through her son's thick curls.

"I'll bet you wish these were her hands running through your hair!" she said.

"You can go ahead and laugh," she said, and he did, both of them giggling for two minutes, as she threw a piece of apple at him, which he caught and ate in a animated way, smacking and licking his lips at her.

CIGARETTES & THIEVES

Alfardo looked at the foul Paulo as they crouched in the backyard of the home, waiting for the couple to leave the house.

The security light brightly lit the images of the elderly man with a cane and a younger woman leaving their home. She inserted the key in the door, checked that it was locked and walked with the man down the stairs as she put him in the car.

"I don't want to go, I'm tired tonight," he said.

"You'll enjoy yourself, and she came to your birthday party, remember?" she said.

The car started, she backed up and drove slowly down the drive, heading off towards Giulianova.

Paulo took out a cigarette and pulled out his lighter.

Alfardo grabbed it and stuffed it in his pants pocket.

"What the hell are you doing? You don't smoke here; they'll smell it in the house and know we've been there…I told you that," said Alfardo, "and the cigarette butts can be linked to you…they know we were here."

"You think the police are going to look for my cigarette butts? What a joke," said Paulo.

"That's exactly what they do," said Alfardo.

"Screw you and your rules, and I'm not going to sit here, let's go," said Paulo.

Alfardo remembered the rumor Paulo was on heroin and wondered if it was true.

Paulo rose and started walking towards the house.

"What the hell are you doing? We wait for 15 minutes, they might forget something," said Alfardo.

"I'm going in. You can do what you want, you're a woman," said Paulo as he gave the universal up yours sign.

Alfardo thought about just staying where he was but then rose and joined him.

The lock was easy, Paulo definitely was a great lock picker. Alfardo closed and relocked the door, then ran upstairs to look for jewels.

Paulo followed.

"You're supposed to be downstairs," said Alfardo.

"The good stuff is upstairs…there'll be plenty for both of us," said Paulo.

Alfardo heard the crunching of stones, then went to the window to see the car returning.

"They're coming back," said Alfardo.

Paulo pulled up his pant leg and took out a pistol.

Alfardo pushed Paulo against the closet door hard and grabbed the gun.

"You're not supposed to carry a gun, you're not supposed to carry a knife," whispered Alfardo.

"If they have a gun, maybe you'll think different," said Paulo.

They went into the bathroom and stood in the bathtub, each hiding behind the decorative curtains placed to each side.

The two heard the downstairs door open and the rushed footsteps of the woman.

She came up the stairs and walked into the adjoining bedroom. Then the light to the bedroom they were close to went on, and they heard a drawer open, then she was in the closet.

Then she came into the bathroom.

She didn't turn on the light, but Alfardo and Paulo watched as she pulled her dress up to her waist, pulled down her underpants, sat on the toilet, and peed.

She said some garbled words very low, cleared her throat, wiped herself with toilet paper, flushed the toilet, pulled up her underwear, pulled down the dress and walked out, then ran down the stairs, and they heard the door lock.

"What the hell were you thinking? I told you to wait outside," said Alfardo.

"I was thinking I'd like to take her…make her squeal like a pig," said Paulo.

LOVE

Honto peeled a mandarin slowly and meticulously, placing each piece of rind in a little dish, as Alfardo spoke in a quiet, almost whisper to him and his wife, as Guardia stood by the sink drying dishes.

"So he had a gun?" said Honto.

"Yes," said Alfardo, laying the pistol on the table.

Honto looked at the gun, inspecting it.

"It's a policeman's gun, it had a number here," Honto said looking closely, "but it's been filed off. We shouldn't keep this, I'll take care of it," he said, putting it in his pocket.

"He could have killed someone; we don't carry weapons…that's one of the rules," said Alfardo.

"Yes," said Honto, "It's one of the rules."

"And he went into the house early, and I told him not to, and he tried to smoke," said Alfardo.

Guardia brought a bottle of licorice aperitif and 3 little glasses.

"What are we celebrating?," Honto asked.

"Your friendship with important people," she said.

"He's dangerous, he could have gotten me into trouble…us into trouble," said Alfardo.

"But he didn't…because you're smart," said Honto, starting to light a cigarette.

Guardia's hand shot out, grabbing it.

"I'm sorry, I forgot," said Honto. "Someday you will be under the control of a woman, and you will learn of suffering."

"And love," said Guardia.

"Oh yes, and of love, and of making love," said Honto.

There was silence.

"What else?" asked Honto.

"I think that Alvana and I...she's here and I'm here," said Alfardo.

"That's your business," said Honto.

"Stop it," said Guardia to Honto, "You know exactly what he's saying."

"So, now you two are together—two against one," said Honto, looking at the two of them, and pushing his lips out in a mocking pout.

"I will think about it," said Honto, "the girl is part of our family, so if you have her then you are part of the family. This is not something for me to take lightly."

Alfardo was sure that Honto would approve... all he had to do was wait, as Guardia had told him in confidence a few days earlier.

Guardia gave Alfardo a look.

Alfardo spoke, "And Paulo, we need...."

"You worry about love, we'll worry about Paulo," Guardia said as she placed her hand on Honto's shoulder.

Honto sighed, "Someday you will be me, and Alvana will be to you like my wonderful woman here is to me, and on that day you will understand."

Seeing Alfardo did not understand, Honto continued.

"Young Alfardo, everybody has their job to do. Paulo does his, and this and that, and you...you do yours and you stop bad things from happening because you are smart, which is why we have you in the house with us and let you sleep and eat with us, while Paulo sleeps alone or with whores."

Guardia slapped the side of Honto's head playfully.

"She's right, we don't speak of whores in this house," said Honto.

"I will think about you and Alvana, and endure the pressures of my love here," Honto said looking up to his wife, "until I agree with everything my wife says."

She elbowed Honto playfully as he bent over in mocked pain, and then he sat up and said loudly to Alfardo while pointing, "and you, you will think about this…someone of filth like Paulo has value to me, and to her," he said looking at his wife, "and value to you, Alfardo."

GAY

Sister Gena was so short that she had little trouble looking through the peephole into Father Nicola's cottage, as she tried to see the cause of the whimpers and cries from the woman visitor.

"I thought my son just liked pretty things, and he said he liked a girl there, but now I find….Father, I can't even say the words…I'm speechless," the woman said.

"Well, she's been talking for ten minutes, so I don't think she's speechless," thought Father Nicola fighting to keep any trace of a smile from his face.

"What makes you think he's gay?" the priest said.

"I put it all together… his fascination with dolls as a child, his love of bright colors, and he loves to cook," she said.

"Some of the best cooks in the world are men," he said.

"What?" she said.

"I said some of the best cooks in the world are men," the priest repeated.

"As a matter of fact, I'm a marvelous cook myself, so I'll take this opportunity to make you some tea," he added, as he stood and placed his hand on her shoulder and went to the little half sink and put some water in the teapot, then onto the stove.

"And you know, many men enjoy colors. House painters are around colors all day, they're not gay. I still don't see how you concluded your son is gay."

"He works in the flower shoppe, he's 22 and hasn't married, but the girls all love him, and he's gentle..," then she stopped and looked at her lap.

He sat next to her and took her hand, "People can like colors, people can be gentle, people can work in flower shoppes….they can do all these things. Look at our finest musicians, they're feminine in some ways, but certainly they are not gay."

"I saw your son sitting having a cappuccino one day with a lovely young woman. He stroked her hair with his hand, and gave her a kiss," he added.

"You don't think he's gay?," she asked.

"If he hasn't told you he's gay, then I would consider that he is a sensitive man, that's all."

"Don't gay people go to hell?" she asked.

"That's a deep question, and there's some controversy within the church on that. I'm not speaking for the church or stating their formal position, but I don't think we know whether your son is gay, so it's gossip, and neither of the two of us engage in gossip."

"We most certainly do not," she said as a smile came across her face, "I'd love some tea."

Gena's eye lifted from the keyhole in the door, she lifted up her dress and ran back up the walk and the steps of the convent school, entered, and closed the door.

The woman's son was seen holding the hand of the girl from the flower shop as they talked in the piazza soon after, and when they stopped, on occasion she would give him an intimate kiss on his cheek.

GRAPE FESTIVAL

One-by-one, or two-by-two, like a call to Noah's ark, the farmers came in by the small country roads with their tractors to the annual Grape Festival.

Scrubbed clean and freshly painted in green, or orange, or red, based on the manufacturer's original color; as out of place as a tuxedo at a farm picnic, the tractors; new and old, made a signature chug-chug-chug sound as black smoke blew out their exhaust pipes rising high at the front of the tractor.

It was the highlight of the year in Mosciano Sant'Angelo, and around the Piazza were placed the many floats they would pull.

The floats were built on flat wooden trailers, usually with four wheels, commandeered from their work hauling corn or hay. Each had a wooden plank bed on top of the steel frame with a foot high rail all-around made of wood. On top of this common platform, each farmer or team created their display. Some recreated a small house made of reeds with a thatched roof and bunches of grapes hung all around, others built over-sized wine barrels as a prop.

In one of the Piazza stores, the 20 people dressed themselves in period costumes: flowing robes and well-tailored period suits with rich dark reds, or greens, and pointed shoes that stuck out almost 6 inches in front, and elaborate hats held on with flowing waves of sheer fabric, all the vogue in the middle ages or 18th century. They laughed and drank wine and talked of their coming promenade around the Piazza.

A raised stage had been constructed at one end of the Piazza, on which the orchestra would play later, and singers, choirs, guitarists, small bands, and even a harmonica band from Giulianova were scheduled as entertainment.

A young boy, Beccaccei, handsome and son of the brick mason, stood in the round church, a small Michelangelo, practicing the solo he would perform later in the day. His voice rose to a pitch only a woman could normally reach, and then down to a baritone. "He has the voice of a master," his teacher had said. He looked up at the beautiful painting of the boy on the ceiling, and sang to God.

The farmers milled around as they flowed into town on their tractors, and in braggadocio manner, like a dance, they threw the tractors into reverse and roared them into the parking place assigned to them, as a helper guided them like they might an airplane pilot on the tarmac. Each tried to outmaneuver the other, and some would roar into place, squealing their brakes. Other farmers, reflecting their conservative nature, would very deliberately place their tractors carefully where asked with a stony look on their faces.

More and more people came at 8 in the morning until there were hundreds, and then Biagio saw Giuliana step up onto the float at the front of the tractor parade which would travel slowly all through the countryside after circling the Piazza.

Biagio saw his Giuliana—the most beautiful young woman in Mosciano Sant'Angelo in a white dress with blue embroidery around her neck.

He made his way through the mass of friends and townsfolk to his friend, a former teacher who had first suggested Biagio study to become a professor.

Biagio whispered in the man's ear, and happily the man gave his favorite student a hand into the float with Giuliana.

Biagio walked over to her and sat down on the wooden plank. His leg just barely touched hers, but neither spoke.

She smiled and waved at her friends.

Biagio found it hard to speak to her at times like this, she was so beautiful. He was so lucky.

He could see his beloved's lovely brown hair, just less than shoulder length, and full lips and small hands. He breathed in and smelled her, with just a faint hint of some flowered perfume.

He looked at her hands; those small hands which would hold him throughout their lives together, and would cradle their children someday.

She was so strikingly beautiful; so much a completion of his dreams of love.

Biagio's mother saw him sitting next to Giuliana, and she decided to simply watch, not approaching them. It felt like she was watching a romantic movie, but so much more poignant as it was her son who loved the girl.

It was the first time she sensed that her boy was now a man, and the thought crossed her mind for the first time that he would find a woman, ask her to marry him, and have children. It was a new thought, and the feelings it created were new also: a mix of sadness at the end of a time, and happiness to see him in love and embracing his future. In the midst of a crowd's noise, she was alone and quiet in her moment.

Biagio reached up to the canopy of the float and plucked two grapes, putting one quickly in his mouth and the other to Giuliana's lips, which she ate laughing. His former teacher at the back smiled at him and winked.

He let his hand slide down until the back of his hand touched the back of her hand.

She turned and stared into his eyes. She was smiling, just looking at him.

He entwined his fingers with hers, and gently stroked the top of her thumb with his.

They rode for miles, past the many grape and olive groves, up to where they could see the Adriatic Sea, then back down where the water was hidden in the hills.

To Biagio, the intermittent glimpses of the Adriatic Sea seemed like his times seeing his love, Giuliana. There were days he would see her, and he felt her beauty was like the sea, then days when he was among the groves and could not see her, then up again.

He was sure in his heart she was the girl he wanted to marry.

She felt his fingers holding hers and the soft caresses from his hands. She squeezed his hand gently.

"I'm sure he's going to try to kiss me again," thought Giuliana.

Up and down the hills with the entourage of tractors, to the fast popping of the engine the couple rode.

Up ahead at the very front was a single tractor with no float…just a driver in his 50's and a beautiful woman of 25; slender with long hair, angular eyebrows and grey eyes. She stood on the tractor behind the seat of the man, her hands resting on his shoulders. Was she his daughter, a friend, his lover? Her small breasts were clearly outlined through her dress by the wind, and her hair flowed behind her in waves like ripples in a lake behind a paddling goose in a pond on a summer morning.

The man spoke to her and she would speak back, but no sound could be heard of their conversation as the tractors combined in a cacophony of rhythmic beats.

When the procession had ended in the Piazza, Biagio helped Giuliana off the float.

"Let's get some popcorn," she said.

"Great, let's do that," said Biagio, and the two worked their way through the throng of people, but he was careful not to hold her hand because just walking together was enough to get the town's gossip mill running at full strength.

The gossip mill: many a visitor came to Mosciano and spoke of the wonders of small town life. Yes, everyone knows each other by name, they know their family's history, where they live, and what family members did for a living back at least two generations.

But what is not seen is the massive spider web of gossip, where every single action of everyone in town is the food for gossip, like hungry goldfish in a tank nibbling at bread.

Who had lunch with whom, who talked to whom, who went for a ride to the beach, who got a job, who got a new coat, and whose relatives were coming from America.

All for the gossip mill.

Another unseen pothole was that if you incurred the town's displeasure, you would be shunned.

Getting a good girl pregnant, especially if the man was older would do that. Violence against a child would do that, or constant rudeness, or drunkenness.

Once snubbed, a mark would be upon you like a scarlet letter; you would walk through town and none of the faces would greet you, they'd look straight ahead.

People who live in a city have no knowledge of this, but in a small town it is an unseen entity; like oxygen in the air. It affects everyone, but you can't see it.

In the midst of this web, and passing many hundreds of people, Biagio made his way with Giuliana to the popcorn.

Handing her the popcorn, he asked, "Did you enjoy my letter?"

She nodded, "Yes, I told you, I read it a lot."

"Well, I meant every word of it," he said looking into her eyes.

"I know you do," she said.

She handed the bag of popcorn to him.

"No, you keep it," he said.

"I have to go," she said and walked off quickly towards her home just two blocks away.

After a few steps, she turned, "Thank you for the popcorn, and…," she didn't know what to say, so just ran her hand through her hair, and waved and skipped off again quickly to her home.

He watched her for a long time, until she turned left down the side street to her house.

The young boy, Beccaccei, was on stage, and an accordion began to play. He sang a student's song, which was a rising and falling of notes, like a piano might do. All the notes were connected like threads in a knitted shawl, each in exactly the place it should be, and the song rose like a gentle hill surrounding Mosciano, and then fell, to rise once again.

One by one, the voices stopped talking, and soon the entire Piazza was quiet, listening to the boy, but for the one man who was laughing and smoking a cigarette at the back of the Piazza.

"Do you mind," said another man, darting his eyes to the young man singing.

The man with the cigarette shrugged his shoulders and walked up to the man who had spoken to him.

"He sings like an angel," said the man with the cigarette, "want a smoke?"

"Yes, thank you," and the two stood and blew the smoke into the air, seeing it dissipate and then disappear entirely.

A KISS AT THE BEACH

Only a faint gentle breeze blew from the Adriatic Sea in the small seaside town of Giulianova just a few miles from Mosciano Sant'Angelo. Biagio, Giuliana, and Silvia lay in the blue and white-striped woven cloth recliner chairs by the waterside in the sun, which felt like an oven set on medium hot.

The beach attendant had offered them a fill up on lemonade twice so just cast an occasional glance.

"What a body on that babe," thought the attendant. "She looks like Sophia Loren, but better."

It didn't matter what Giuliana wore, she was sexy.

The attention of men was so constant now she'd accepted the fact that her body was the major part of what people saw her for being. And like all beautiful women, she both appreciated and resented the attention.

It bothered her that men took so little time to understand her thoughts and feelings, but always just stared at her, and the attention of young men sometimes felt like an insult.

She and Biagio saw that Silvia's hand had gone limp, and heard little snoring sounds, so Biagio took her chin gently in his palm and gave her a light kiss on the lips.

They went to the water's edge, then in over their ankles, and kicked the water gently at each other, laughing.

She loved the way he touched her, always so gentle, and he never went where he was not supposed to go, where a good girl wouldn't let a young man go.

They ran back to their chairs, Biagio was thankful Silvia was still asleep as he pulled the waist of his shorts away from him to let the water escape, then lay on the chair.

Giuliana thought, "I can't believe I love Biagio so much, I didn't' think it was possible to love a person this much."

She was totally devoted to him, her heart completely his.

Her hand tousled his hair, exactly as she'd seen his mother do to him so many times, and she tapped the tip of his nose with her finger tip.

That night, Biagio lay in bed thinking of those moments, and his thoughts and dreams were like ecstasy.

DIARY

She wrote, "I cannot believe I love Biagio so much, it seems so little time since I was a little girl, and now a man tells me he loves me with all his heart."

Why does he love me? What does he see?

I dream of his kisses, and almost shake when he's close to me.

I didn't think it was possible to love a person this much.

Her hand caressed the carved wood of the diary's cover, and her fingertips felt the coolness of the metal casting of Christ on the cross.

Three years later…

VINCE'S EYES

Vince DiPasquale at 26 was nice-looking, masculine and muscular with thick dark hair and eyes which focused on things like a bird or a hawk might.

Born in Mosciano Sant'Angelo, he apprenticed as a mechanic with a bus company there, and at 18 moved to America to join his mother to work as a mechanic.

He had returned to Mosciano Sant'Angelo just this once in 1956 to visit his home town and spend time with his father, his sisters and family, and friends including Piero, the son of the shop owner where Vince had apprenticed.

Vince came to the one-story shop made of grey painted concrete block and saw the transmission components strewn like dropped toothpicks on the garage floor.

"You should have put those on newspaper, not the floor," said Vince to Piero.

"The mechanic is sick, but he said he's sorry he took it apart because he can't get it back together," said Piero.

"C'mon, let's get a cappuccino," Vince said.

The two walked to the Piazza.

"You don't talk much about your mother, why?" asked Piero lighting a cigarette. "You still don't smoke, huh?"

Vince answered, "My mother, she was born in Italy, grew up in America; she's an American, and my father grew up in Italy, but immigrated to America with my mother."

"I knew about that," said Piero.

"Then they decided to leave America and buy a farm in Italy," said Vince.

"Why did she leave her all her kids she'd raised in Italy and go back to America?" asked Piero.

"She didn't like working on the farm; she didn't like the work or the life. She'd deliver milk to Mosciano. One day when I was 15, after she'd had 11 kids, my mother decided to go home to America, and I joined her after 3 years."

"How did you feel about it?," asked Piero.

"Any time someone moves, it's hard, but the other kids felt abandoned. I didn't like it, but I was older," said Vince. "My sisters, especially, were upset. Mother writes to them, but…," and Vince just stopped talking.

They sat at the small table and Vince's eyes caught a beautiful young woman. She was, not exaggerating, the most beautiful girl he'd ever seen in his life. His mouth actually opened as he stared at her: dark eyes, shoulder length hair, an absolutely beautiful face, and when she walked it was like a thousand dancers moving in unison.

"What?" said Piero.

"That girl," said Vince.

"That's Giuliana, you know her."

"Impossible, she was just 10 years old when I was here last, it can't be her," Vince said.

The talk about Giuliana went on and on until Piero insisted they return to the shop where Vince knelt down on one knee inspecting the transmission parts.

"You can't put this transmission back together…you've never seen it before," said Piero.

"Tell me more about the girl, and I'll help you with this," said Vince as his small fingers rolled each of the wet parts, sliding them all quickly together like a puzzle, rebuilding half the transmission in minutes.

Piero took his time, telling him all about the girl, her father Gennaro, and the shoppe her mother ran, but he waited until the last of the transmission was complete to tell Vince,

"She lives just across the street there," he said pointing.

"Vince, I hate to tell you this, but you don't have a chance. She's got a boyfriend; he wants to marry her, and you're 10 years older than her. Her mother will never go for it, and…she's a Grilli."

"She has a boyfriend?" Vince said looking up, "Not for long."

Vince completed the transmission, and was happy to work with Piero every day from then on, always keeping an eye on Giuliana's home.

She might come out, and his eyes would feast on the food of centuries of men who dreamed of a beautiful woman in their arms—a possession—theirs to have and take.

WATCHING

Vince helped Piero each day, always looking over at the girl's home. When he saw Giuliana come of out of her house, he would clean his hands and run after her.

Again and again, he'd follow her, walking half a block behind, and when she sat or entered a store, he'd go up and talk with her, or stand near her.

One day she'd had enough.

"Stop following me, why are you following me?" she said, her eyes hot.

"I like you, I want….to get to know you," he said.

"You're an American, I'm not interested in Americans," she said laughing, "You wear brown shoes with grey pants. Americans don't know how to dress. I have a boyfriend and I'm not interested, so stop following me. How old are you?" she asked.

"I'm 26, but I have a good job in America, I'm a good mechanic," he said.

"I know who you are, I've seen you. You're too old for me, and I'm not interested," and she walked away without saying goodbye.

THE STORE

Vince had been rebuffed, but doubled his efforts, focusing on Giuliana's mother.

He went to the store every day when he knew boxes were delivered, to ask if he could help.

Wearing a T-shirt showing his muscles, he would pick up crates and boxes of goods delivered for the store and help stock the shelves, get change from the bank, or watch the store for a moment while Silvia ran an errand.

Silvia had known him most of his life, until he went to America, and was mildly amused by his infatuation with her daughter.

"Giuliana has a boyfriend," Silvia said one day.

"I know, but people like you and me, we are hard workers and both strong," he said with a wink.

Silvia let him do all the work he was willing to do and he never asked for any money, but instead spent it on things like ice cream for Silvia, and he always had a large bundle of paper money in his pocket which he'd take out and count so she could see it.

MISSING THE BOAT

Vince knew that he would have to stay in Italy a bit longer to win Giuliana or lose her forever, so he cancelled his boat trip home on the passenger liner, the Andrea Doria.

Days later Vince read the headline in the newspaper, "ANDREA DORIA SINKS IN NANTUCKET, COLLIDES WITH OTHER SHIP."

He walked slowly to the shop and showed Piero the paper.

"Looks like that girl saved your life," said Piero.

And that was how Vince interpreted it…a sign that he'd done the right thing to risk all to win Giuliana's love.

FIGHT

"I want you to leave my girlfriend alone," Biagio said to Vince, while two of Biagio's friends stood nearby.

"It's a free country," said Vince, "and you're not married. You want to start a fight, start a fight. I'm a tourist, and you cause trouble with a tourist in Italy, you could end up in jail," said Vince.

Vince taunted him in other ways, telling another friend visiting from America in English, "I'm going to marry that guy's girlfriend," pointing to Biagio, but Biagio spoke no English and could not understand his words.

LOSING THE HOUSE

Silvia sat reading the letter from her sister-in-law, over and over, fixated.

The trumpet playing stopped from the upstairs room, and Gennaro came down.

He had not seen this look on his wife's face before, "What's wrong?"

"This letter, my sister-in-law says she wants us to buy the house," said Silvia.

"She said she would never sell the house," he said.

"Well, she wants to sell the house and she wants us to buy it."

"Can we do that?" he asked.

"It's more, much more than she paid. She said the house is worth more now…and we were stupid enough to put money into it every year. Now we have to pay more."

"Maybe she'll let us pay a little bit every month, let's ask her," Gennaro said.

"No, she wants the money, and we can't go to the bank because the store is a cash business, and she has another buyer interested," said Silvia.

"Let me deal with it," said Silvia, "I'll come up with something…. don't worry yourself, you have a performance tonight. I'll figure it out."

As Gennaro walked up the stairs, he stopped to view the photo in the stairway from their marriage day. *"Your wife has a good head for business, and that's good for a talented artist like you,"* his father had said of Silva.

"She's just the kind of woman who's a good choice for you…you're smarter than I thought," his father had said.

And his father had been right; from the house, to the store, to the loans to friends, Silvia always came out on top.

He felt pleased and secure in the decision he'd made to marry such a strong woman with such a good head for business.

His wife would work it out, she always did.

VINCE'S DREAM

Giuliana became a fixation for Vince; if he didn't see her every day he became depressed.

Then he had a dream, and he had never dreamed of a woman before.

In the dream, he had an argument with Giuliana, she was furious with him, and Silvia said to him in the dream, "You're not going to have my daughter."

Vince was so upset he went to Silvia's store the next day and told her the whole story.

"But you're not dating my daughter, she has a boyfriend; Biagio," said Silvia.

"I know, I know, but I love your daughter and I want to marry her and take her back to America," Vince said.

Silvia eyed him, and said, "I need to get back to work."

"You've got to help me. I'll help you. I'm not poor," he said.

"It was just a dream," Silvia said.

"Cannot a dream become true?" he asked, "I live in America, with a house, and she'll have money," he said, exaggerating the truth.

Silvia stopped laughing and stared at him.

NIGHT

Giuliana stood near the heavy dark wooden door at the top of the stairs of her family's home, opening it an inch to hear what the animated discussion was about. Her parents never argued loudly.

Silvia said, "I told you before, she wants the money for the house—we either buy it or we have to move."

"Well then, let's buy it, that's the thing to do," answered Gennaro.

"Buy it, just buy it? With what? We don't have any savings; we put everything into the house, and all we did was to make the house worth more, and now we have to pay more because it's worth more. We should have left it a pig's sty," said Silvia.

"I'm sure if you talk to your sister-in-law…" interjected Gennaro.

"I have. She said she wants the money," Silvia said.

"Well then, if we can't buy it—we can't buy it, so we move," said Gennaro.

"The American boy, Vince DiPasquale, he says he loves Giuliana. Maybe he will help us. Maybe we can work something out with him to save the house. Americans always have money," said Silvia.

"But Biagio is her boyfriend, he loves her…," said Gennaro.

Then the voices grew hushed.

Giuliana closed the door and tiptoed to her bedroom and lay in bed.

All night long she thought about what she'd heard.

"What am I going to do? I'm in love with Biagio," she thought.

"I know my father doesn't want to leave this house."

"Where are we supposed to go? We can't leave the house, it's our home."

THE BEGINNING

"How do you feel about Vince?," Silvia asked the next morning.

"I don't know, I love Biagio," answered Giuliana.

"You don't know Vince well enough to know if you like him or not," said Silvia.

Then both were silent.

THE DEAL IN GIULIANOVA

Vince and Silvia met in a small café in Giulianova.

A friend of a woman who ran the dress shoppe in Mosciano saw them from two tables down, curious on what the two could be up to.

Silvia said, "I'm not hungry," to the waiter.

Deeply upset, she began, "So we need to do something to keep the house, or the house goes to sale, and in Italy we don't do that: the homes stay in the family and are passed down generation after generation, a cherished heirloom in the family."

Vince was not educated, but he knew what opportunity looked like, "If I were married to Giuliana, then I would want her to live in that home. I could help pay for it, and it would be ours someday anyway, then that would be the right thing to do," he said.

Silvia liked his cleverness, "But she has a boyfriend," she said.

He put a piece of lightly pan fried calamari to his lips, and shrugged his shoulders.

His next question was the telling one as he stared into her eyes like a gambler in a high stakes poker game, "How much money do you need?"

"Five thousand dollars…you pay half," said Silvia.

"That's not a problem," he said. "Suppose a man could provide fifteen hundred dollars cash now and pay the rest over a few years, you think that would do?"

Silvia nodded yes.

"Then we have a deal, and I have a new mother-in-law who I will make happy, and a wife who will be the happiest woman in the world, in America, where everyone's dreams come true," he said as he lifted a wine glass.

She lifted hers slowly and tapped his glass then drank, as the two stared at each other.

Silvia's appetite had returned, and she glanced at the waiter. She picked up the wine menu to search for her favorite, a Rosé, and ordered the large seafood platter.

"Get anything you want," said Vince.

A PLEASANT START

Silvia had made Giuliana's favorite dish of pasta with pan-fried chicken, and sat with her holding her hand.

"I know you love Biagio, but you know, there are other men. Maybe you should date some others while you still can. You're single, enjoy life."

"I'm not interested in other men," Giuliana said.

"At your age, it's ok to see two men, and you don't have an engagement ring." (The only reason Giuliana did not have an engagement ring being that Silvia had forbidden Biagio to give her one as a condition of seeing her daughter.)

"Then you can be sure who you care for," said Silvia.

Giuliana stopped eating and put her fork down.

"Don't pout," said Silvia putting her hands on Giuliana's plate to take it away, "finish your meal or I'll throw it away."

DIARY

I am so confused I cannot even think.

My mother attacks Biagio every day, more and more and more, it never stops, but I know I love him.

It's my choice, it's my choice to make, not hers. I am the one who loves Biagio and he loves me.

Why doesn't my father help me?

Jesus, I pray you make my mother stop, she must stop.

My life would not be life without Biagio's love.

HAVING TO WAIT TEN YEARS

The criticisms of Biagio from Silvia came on slowly at first, then more and more frequently with more aggression, like bullets from a machine gun tearing at her every day.

"Biagio is not a good choice for you. He still has many more years before he can marry. He has to finish college, and then more schooling after that to be a professor. You'll be too old. You should listen to your mother, we know better than you. We are your parents," said Silvia.

Giuliana said nothing, but simply looked at her hands in her lap.

"His grandfather was unkind to his wife, is that the kind of man you want?" she said.

Silvia continued, "But Vince, he is from America, with money, and he's a hard worker, and from Mosciano. You'd have a good life in America like the life I always dreamed of."

"My biggest regret was not moving to America, as my sister did," Silvia added.

Gennaro heard her statement, laid the newspaper down without speaking and quietly left the house.

Silvia continued with her comments and attacks, ignoring everything Giuliana said until Giuliana left the house or went to her room.

Then the next time Silvia had her cornered, she started the whole process over and over again.

Like a water torture….drip, drip, drip.

LEA'S HOME

"Tell him to stop following you then," said Lea.

Giuliana looked out Lea's front window for her mother, "She's coming back. I can't stay long. She's driving me nuts. Vince this, Vince that," said Giuliana.

"And I did tell Vince to stop following me, so did Biagio, but he just ignores us and tries to start a fight with Biagio to get him into trouble," Giuliana added.

"I don't want us to lose the house," Giuliana said in a whisper.

Lea took Giuliana's face in her hands, "My dearest Giuliana, do not pick the man you are to marry for a house…marry the man you love. You have to decide which man you love—in your heart."

Giuliana heard the words of her friend, and appreciated that she cared.

But when she thought about her own needs, or what was in her interest, it just felt like an ocean-sized void or emptiness with no form, no borders, and no answers.

She didn't know if it was because of the convent school, or her mother's statements about her being born to make her sister die, or something else.

Giuliana bent forward, with her face in her lap.

Lea looked out the window, "Here comes your mother."

LEA'S TALK WITH SILVIA

"What are you thinking?" Lea said to Silvia later in the day as the two sat in Silvia's kitchen.

"Biagio is not the boy for her. She should go to America…she'll have a better life," said Silvia.

Lea looked at her friend, and felt pity.

"She should marry the man she loves. You've always said you didn't go to America because you didn't want to leave Gennaro, but that's exactly what you are doing to her. She's your only daughter, do you want to be alone in your old age?" said Lea.

"Giuliana has no sense, she doesn't know who she loves. Biagio is just a crush, Vince has a trade and he's a man. Giuliana will decide," said Silvia.

Many things went through Lea's mind which she did not say, as she valued their friendship.

And Silvia thought of suggesting Lea run her family, and Silvia would run hers, but for once was silent.

So Lea kissed Silvia's cheek and left.

HAMMER

Biagio knocked on the door of Giuliana's home with books in hand, as he had done many times.

He would sit at the kitchen table with Giuliana and they would do homework, or read in the living room side-by-side, with the backs of their hands touching.

Biagio smiled as Silvia opened the door.

"Giuliana's not here," said Silvia as Biagio started telling her about a grade he'd received, but she closed the door in his face.

"Sit down," Silvia told Giuliana, as she pointed to the kitchen table.

Giuliana hoped this would not be another lecture on the plusses of Vince and the faults of Biagio.

"You are not going to date Biagio any more; he's not coming to the house. You are not to see him or talk with him."

Giuliana started to speak, Silvia interjected, "Don't interrupt me. Biagio is not the one for you."

"I'm not interested in Vince," Giuliana said, as she stuck her tongue between her teeth, biting lightly.

"Stop biting your tongue, or I'll slap you," said Silvia.

"You are too young to know what is best for you, and you do like Vince. I've seen that you smile at him, and he's very nice to you," Silvia added.

"You will have nothing here in Italy…in America, everything. All my life I wanted to go to America," said Silvia.

Gennaro walked into the kitchen, then left abruptly climbing the stairs to their bedroom, and soon the sounds of his arpeggio scales could be heard muted from above.

"My sister went to America and she has everything. It's not up to you;

you are part of the family and we have to decide what is best for you and in your interest," her mother said.

"You said a young woman can see two men," said Giuliana, who so far had only gone on two walks with Vince to silence her mother.

"That was then. If you don't stay with Vince, he'll think you were leading him on," her mother said.

Giuliana was frozen. She knew that any word from her would just result in more and more babble from her mother.

It was always the same: first a small lecture, then longer and longer. Her mother never listened, not once in her life, not to a word. One time Giuliana had just said the word "lemon" when her mother was in one of her fits talking—just to see what would happen. Her mother never missed a beat but just continued as before.

Giuliana's mind stopped functioning and she could no longer hear the words her mother said, it was just lips moving, and Giuliana knew that no matter what she did, her mother would have her way.

If there was a part of her that could speak for her own interests, she didn't know it. If there was a part of her that could stand up to her mother, she had not found it.

In bed that night, Giuliana heard her parents talking in low mumbles. It was like she was listening to a low rumbling thunder coming her way on a rainy day. The words came and went, rumbled and then stopped.

Thoughts came to her and left.

A daughter is to be obedient to her parents in the same way we are obedient to Christ. What good is a daughter who does not honor her parents? What is her place then?

All the lessons, and words, and values spoken over and over again from childhood surrounded her like a mist and one by one assailed her.

But a part of her could not let go…

And then she thought that perhaps she should kill herself.

If I die, then I won't have to go with Vince, she thought.

But she knew the teachings of the church, and suicide was an unpardonable sin.

"I cannot do that," she said.

Her diary—she could tell the truth in the diary…her truth, always and forever.

"Do I really love Biagio? Yes, I do. But so much seems unclear to me. I don't want to get married, I'm happy at school, I like my friends."

"How do I really feel about Vince? He's cute and he's very nice to me, and he's strong."

"But…it should be *my* choice who I love, shouldn't it? I've only seen Vince for three weeks, what am I to know or understand of someone in that short a time?"

"It doesn't matter what I do, or say, my mother will have her way. I don't remember one time, just one time, she didn't get her way. All my life, every day, it's her way."

"I could refuse, I could tell her, no, I love Biagio, and I'm going to do that."

"And what then? My parents will have to leave the house. Where will they go? Where will they eat, and where would my father practice trumpet?"

She prayed to God and to Jesus Christ to help her.

Her life was a mess of contradictions, like a swirling mass of grays and whites, coming in on itself, and she saw it like a motion picture before her eyes…movement and feelings of fear, being lost, and she felt a tear fall from her eye and make its way slowly down her cheek.

She wiped it with the palm of her hand, "Well, there's no use arguing with my mother, that I know."

"But I don't really know Vince. Before I get too upset I can get to know him, and if I can't stand him I can run away, or go to the priest and become a nun."

The diary was done, so she lay for a long while trying to fall to sleep, which finally came.

GUILIANA AGAIN ASKS FOR A GARDEN

For ten years straight, Giuliana had asked her father for a garden.

Giuliana showed the photo of the plans from the magazine to her father two mornings later.

"See it has blues, and yellows, and these tall things."

"We don't have room for a garden with flowers," he said, looking up from polishing his trumpet.

"We don't eat flowers," he said, "and there's no room because we have tomatoes, peppers, and zucchini in our food garden."

"We do have room, right out near the end of the front yard, close to the street, near the cement laundry tub. We could make a little garden with flowers. Oh please," she said.

"I don't have time for a flower garden," he said, not unkindly.

VITTORIA'S DIARY

Her finger tips peered into the recesses of the carved leaf pattern stained a dark walnut with a hint of mahogany red.

She saw again, in the center of the diary's cover the metal casting of Jesus on the cross.

"Jesus, I know you see what I write, I know you do."

She poured her feelings into the diary, every drop of ink a drop of her life.

Her story would be known, people in the future would know, it would be a permanent record so everyone would know her truth.

Thousands of years from now, someone would see, maybe one would even care.

She wrote this sentence many times, like a child at a blackboard...

"I am being forced into dating a man I do not love."

THE GYPSY TANGO

Honto was out of town, and Guardia had said they would go to a dance with rough Hungarians who would be in town, that she knew someone.

It was a dark bar in a home outside of town, and as they walked in, the men smoking nodded to Guardia, and blew their smoke away from her.

Vodka and beer were thrust at them, and Alfardo could not take his eyes off of Alvana.

Her long dark hair hung straight down to her mid-back, with red lipstick, and a dress with a slit on the right side, where just a hint of her thigh was visible.

The Tango music started, as the pulsating thump and hesitations of the bandoneon began.

"Take her, take her to dance," said Guardia.

His arms were around her back and he could feel her muscles and bone, and the slight dampness of her body.

He breathed in and felt her odor, fresh, clean, and tasted a hint of her perfume.

His idea of dancing was simply to hold her against his body and writhe, but she began to dance and it was clear she knew the Tango.

She posed and kicked her leg in the air, and lifted it to crook it around his lower back.

He looked down to see her exposed thigh against his body, and tried to pull her to him to kiss her on her lips.

She stepped away, and turned a pirouette or circle in place, then pushed her breasts into his chest, and pressed the front of her body against his, and slid her body touching his, up and down.

His breath escaped like steam from a teapot.

She taunted him with her sexuality for most of half an hour.

He was quite out of his mind, with Guardia eying them both with the gentle gaze, and all would have thought Alfardo was her son, had they not known better.

ROOM

Biagio sat in his room with his head hung down, staring at the page in his textbook. He stared and stared, but did not turn the page.

He would try to read a word and then become lost.

Then a knock at the door.

His mother entered.

"Why didn't you eat dinner?"

"I don't feel well," he said.

"You mean you miss her," she said, "Silvia won't let you in the house?"

"She just closes the door and says Giuliana is not at home, but I know she is," said Biagio.

"What about town; have you seen her in the Piazza?" asked his mother.

"She doesn't go there anymore," he said.

The mother took her son's hand and held it, then took the book from him and closed it, "Well, come and eat, and we'll talk and see if there isn't something to be done."

STORE TALK

"We need to talk, you and I," said Biagio's mother to Silvia in the store.

"What is there to talk about, she's not interested in Biagio," said Silvia.

"This isn't a card game, Silvia, I know you…I've known you since you were a little girl. That's not what's going on. The two of them are in love, Biagio wants to marry Giuliana."

"Everybody wants to marry Giuliana because she's a beautiful young woman. Biagio is just another boy; he was her first love, that's it," said Silvia.

Biagio's mother eyed Silvia, and could sense the woman was lying, or at least that she wasn't telling the whole truth.

She thought of many things she could say: that Silvia was selfish, that she was a liar, that she was ignorant, more man than woman, or cruel for breaking her son's heart.

Or she could appeal to young love, and ask for some way to make things right.

She wanted to say that she'd find out the truth and tell everyone—but she knew for a certainty that for whatever reason Silvia did this, nothing she could say would make any difference whatever, so she left the store without saying goodbye.

BIAGIO'S MOTHER AT LEA'S HOME

Biagio's mother sat before Lea and told her the entire story.

"I know something of this," said Lea, offering her more cappuccino.

"I've had enough, thank you. What will I do Lea?"

"I don't know what to say," Lea replied.

"Yes, you know what to say," interjected Biagio's mother, "but you won't tell me. I know Giuliana is like your daughter; you know she loves my son, and you know why Silvia is doing this. At least tell me that."

Lea knew if she told this woman about the money for the house, it would end her friendship with Silvia forever, and much worse—Silvia would keep her from speaking to her darling Giuliana for years…maybe a lifetime.

Forcing Giuliana to marry a man for money to buy their home was so inappropriate an action for Silvia and Gennaro to take that it might even affect Gennaro's impeccable reputation, and could even affect Giuliana's position in the small town life.

The town's judgment could be severe and immediate.

Lea felt the weight that many people do when they carry the burden of the truth but know that if they share it, many people will be hurt, so it sits in them like a stone.

"I know, I know," said Biagio's mother, "you can't tell me because it would betray a confidence."

"But you know she is a hard-headed woman, and I'll tell you this," said Biagio's mother, "whatever happens won't be good for the girl. She's the pawn on the chessboard, and Silvia cheats at cards so you figure it out."

She rose, set down her cup and kissed Lea on the cheek.

"I'm not mad at you. You'd have told me if you could, I just needed to talk with someone…so, now you're in the middle."

She walked home slowly thinking how she would break her son's heart, and never in her wildest imaginings did she think her life would come to this.

Her son was a perfect young man, and the only good she could see was that Silvia would not be a part of her family, and of that fact she was glad, and thankful.

"How Gennaro picked her is beyond me," she said under her breath.

But Lea spoke to people in town of this injustice to more than a few sympathetic ears, and the birds on the wire saw Biagio's head hung in sadness, and they had all known heartbreak, so understood too well. The town saw the American with his energetic walk and his great love for Giuliana, but for the first time in Silvia's life, the fish bowl of town gossip began to turn on her.

It would have been far worse had Silvia not lent money to so many, but she had, and she was more generous in the months to come, allowing more time for repayment than in years past.

BIAGIO SICK

He had felt sick to his stomach for three days, unable to eat, and peculiar for him, uninterested in his studies.

Every day, he looked for Giuliana.

Silvia no longer even provided him the courtesy of answering the door when he knocked. Giuliana was nowhere to be seen…it was impossible, how do you hide a girl in a town of only 3500 people, and worse, Giuliana went to the back of the store if Biagio came in the store to see her.

He went over what had happened again and again.

Was she mad because he kissed her on the beach when her mother was asleep? How did Giuliana's mother learn about it? What was Giuliana's mother thinking?

"I just want to know what happened, what to do," he thought.

His mother knocked at his bedroom door, and entered sitting on the side of his bed.

"I went to see Silvia, but she didn't say anything. I know this is not Giuliana's doing, I am absolutely positive," Biagio's mother said.

"I know Giuliana cares for you, but you know Silvia, she can be…." and she stopped talking.

He didn't say a word.

"Sometimes there is nothing you can do in life but just wait for something to change," Biagio's mother said.

She went to the door and turned, "When you love someone, the price you pay is pain—it comes with loving someone, sometimes. And I am so sad to say this to you, sometimes you have to move on from a terrible and tragic situation because it's the only thing one can do," she said blowing him a kiss.

One by one, she asked the people in the town what had happened, the same questions were asked over and over. No one knew, but she knew she'd find the answer eventually, "I just hope it's in time to do something."

Whatever it was had to be bad, or worse, or Lea would have told her. She would ask Lea again and again a million times if she had to, eventually she'd have to tell.

VITTORIA'S DIARY ENTRY

Sometimes I wonder where the "me" is in my life.

My mother tells me I can no longer see Biagio. How can she do that?

I hear the sounds of my father's trumpet, and everyone's life flows around me, but I do not feel life.

When will my feelings be seen?

When will someone ask how I feel…about anything?

Giuliana became afraid and stopped.

FRIENDS

The transmission was coming back together; Vince put the parts in place and screwed in the perfectly machined bolts while his friend held the parts.

"I thought the mechanic was coming back," said Vince.

"No, his father is still sick, so we count on you," Piero said, "and you get the view of Giuliana's house," he said laughing.

"So, how did you get rid of her boyfriend?" asked Piero.

"I did what it took," answered Vince.

"I thought you were kidding when you said it wouldn't be long until she was yours. They were a couple—he was going to marry her, he told me so."

"We gotta get the two big gears," said Vince as they walked to the side of the garage.

"We still have to clean them," said Piero.

"I did that this morning while you were sleeping," said Vince.

They lifted the parts and brought them over to the canvas cover on the floor, next to the frame brace holding the transmission, before it was to be dropped back into the drivetrain of the truck.

"Guys don't understand women," said Vince. "Guys don't have any confidence, so they don't tell the girl they love them, and then the girl doesn't know, and they go with some other guy who has the guts to say they love them. Most guys are too afraid to take the chance."

"Dating a woman is like a dance. You know how to dance, right Piero? You move forward, you move back. You don't know how to dance, do you?" asked Vince.

Piero shook his head, "No."

"She'll let you know when she wants you to move. Women like men who can dance, see I can dance, it shows them how you work with people," said Vince, "and dress sharp, men don't know how to dress right… they should learn. We want girls to look good, but we look like slobs. Don't do that."

"I thought the men lead in dancing," said the friend.

Vince held up the open ended wrench, waving it, "Naw, naw, they just think they're leading. Women control everything."

Vince saw that Piero didn't understand, "I'm just saying in a relationship with a girl, she lets you know what she wants."

Vince continued, "But guys don't listen…they're always trying to have sex. And the other hint I'll give you is to be nice to parents, real nice, because they're with the girl all the time, and they get something in their head and it's gonna get through to the girl. So be nice and give 'em reasons to like you," said Vince.

"What kind of reasons?" asked Piero.

"Whatever they want," said Vince.

"And I'll tell you this…you got to keep your hands off the girl, cause they don't want to be pressured. If a girl wants you to kiss her, she'll let you know," he said.

"How?" said Piero.

Vince just laughed, as he saw Pierro knew as little of women as he did about transmission repair.

"I don't think it's possible to win Giuliana…what you did, it can't be done," said Piero.

"It can't be done by you," said Vince.

"It's like this wrench…you gotta have skills to fix a machine, and skills to get a woman. I gave you a lot of good advice, and I didn't charge you anything," said Vince.

"Let me give you some other advice while I'm helping you out," said Vince, "Women don't like men who tell other guys about how the girl kisses them. It insults them, and if they find out you're in trouble."

"She's a virgin now, and she's gonna be a virgin when I marry her," said Vince.

"Did you kiss her or not?" asked Piero.

"You don't learn," said Vince as he looked down and worked.

"I still don't see how you got her," said Piero, "she's the most beautiful girl for hundreds of miles, and you're just kind of average, no offense."

"It's not about looks, I'm good looking enough and I'm shorter, but I got guts, and she likes that. Her parents like that."

"You see something in life—you take it…people respond to that, it's basic. The parents figure the guy who sticks with it to win their daughter's heart might be the right one for her. They don't want a quitter. Girls too. They want to see you sweat, they want to see what you do when you struggle," said Vince.

"You watch me work on cars and trucks…you'll learn about cars, you watch me with Giuliana…you'll learn about getting the girl you want," said Vince.

"I drive the bus, I'm not a mechanic," said Piero.

"Yeah, and you're not marrying Giuliana," said Vince.

"I don't see a ring on her finger, not yet," said Piero.

Vince just looked up.

"How'd you learn all this?," asked Piero.

"My mother told me," said Vince, "and she told me to get back to work. Then we'll get some lunch."

"If Giuliana doesn't come out," said Piero looking towards the girl's house.

THE PRIEST'S COTTAGE

Sister Gena watched from the window of the school until Biagio's mother left the priest, and then she walked quickly on the path to the priest's cottage and knocked softly.

"It's open, please come in," he said.

He was pleased to see it was his Gena.

"Would you like tea, my little angel?" he asked as a brother might to his sister.

She shook her head no.

He waved her to a chair, "I do, so I hope you won't mind," he said as he put the water on.

Looking at her with a soft smile he said, "You're not being nosy, you know…you raised Giuliana."

The priest began, "Biagio's mother says something is wrong; Giuliana is not allowed to see Biagio at all, and the young American, Vince DiPasquale, is seeing her all the time."

He looked at Sister Gena waiting for her to speak.

"Nothing to say?" he asked.

"If I don't have anything good to say, then I say nothing," Sister Gena said.

"Biagio's mother wants me to find out what happened, but she doesn't know Silvia," he said dipping the teabag in the water.

"It really doesn't matter why that woman does what she does, and knowing it won't do you any good," added the priest.

"Well, at least she has two men who love her," said Sister Gena looking at her lap.

"That will cause her more pain than she knows," said the priest as he handed her the tea, which she accepted sweetly.

GENNARO AND SILVIA IN BED

"Silvia, are you awake?" asked Gennaro, as he lay unable to sleep at 2 in the morning.

"What?" she answered.

"One of the orchestra members said a woman told him you are forcing Giuliana to go with Vince."

"It's a lie," she said.

"You told me it was her choice to go with Vince, that you didn't force her. That it's what she wants."

"Biagio is not the one for Giuliana, Vince is a hard worker, and I think he's a better choice, and it will be ten years before Biagio can marry Giuliana, that's way too long," she said.

"He's not her choice," Gennaro said.

Silvia turned over in bed with her back against her husband.

"She's 16 years old, what does she know about what makes her happy? Happy is in America with a future, she's a child in a woman's body. We need to get her married before someone gets her pregnant," Silvia said.

"That's ridiculous, she's just an innocent girl, she's a good girl. You know that. I don't want people saying we forced her to do anything," said Gennaro.

"Do you want to lose the house?" she asked.

"All the blame goes to me, so he can sleep better," she said to herself.

Gennaro thought, "What Silvia says is not true. Biagio is a gentleman, and the woman's right, she is forcing Giuliana. The truth is….," and he stopped. "But what can I do, Silvia will do what she wants to do."

He thought about taking a stand and for the first time in their marriage, telling Silvia to stop, demanding she stop, saying that he was the man in the family and he would decide who his daughter married and who she would not marry. He would stand tall and speak slowly and clearly, and take charge, take control.

But a man must often accept so many things he does not desire if he wants to share a bed with a woman. "I'll talk with Silvia when she's in a more agreeable mood," he said to himself.

So he said nothing, and looked at the grey shapes on the wall by the light of the window through one eye, with the other eye closed, until he fell to sleep.

VINCE ASKS...MARRY ME

Every day, Vince had pestered Giuliana, asking over and over if she would marry him.

He had delayed his trip home and thus avoided the sinking of the liner, Andrea Doria. He'd won her mother over…it was his time and he knew it.

Vince saw her come out of her house and called to her. He walked to the fence at the end of the auto repair shop property.

Giuliana looked at him, and then at her shoes in a fun way.

"You know you're going to say yes, I mean, you know it. I leave tomorrow. Tell me you will marry me so I can be happy and devote my life to you; c'mon, tell me."

"Vince, I've only been seeing you for a few weeks. You go back to America, and you can write to me. When you come next spring I'll give you my answer."

"Well, I think that's a yes," he said smiling at her.

"Don't get your hopes up too high, they might sink like that boat. Wouldn't want to see you get hurt," she said as she skipped away, looking back at him.

"I'm taking that as a yes, I'm taking that as a yes," he yelled after her as she skipped away.

Vince told Silvia that essentially she'd said yes, and all started moving towards a wedding in the spring.

But Giuliana had not said yes, and she had not said no.

THE NOTE TO GIULIANA AND A MEETING

Vince had been gone for two months when Biagio was able to get a note to Giuliana through her little brother, Claudio.

Biagio's note was like a gift from heaven, "I love you. Meet me at my aunt's house today at 1, we need to talk and make plans," she read as her hands trembled.

The knock came at the door as Biagio's aunt opened it.

Biagio gave Giuliana a hug.

"I'm going for a very short walk so the two of you can talk," said his aunt, and she left.

He spoke of his love for her and asked if she loved him, and their love for each other was rekindled in the words they spoke.

Biagio's Aunt walked as quickly as she could to Silvia's store, "He's talking with her at my house, right now."

Silvia ran from the store to the house, entered, and grabbed her daughter by the arm.

"You're leaving right now, I told you, you're not allowed to see him," she said roughly to her daughter. Then to him, "Leave her alone, she has somebody else, behind my back, you see her behind my back?" she said coldly as his mouth fell open and he found he was unable to speak.

Silvia hurt her daughter's arm, "How could you do this? You are leading Vince on, it's indecent."

"I never…" started Giuliana.

But her mother cut her off and pushed her quickly from the home.

And the tears fell from Biagio's face onto the floor of his aunt's home, and the tears of Giuliana fell on the stones.

And Biagio's aunt sat at the store, waiting for Silvia to return, knowing that with Giuliana married to Vince, her daughter could marry Giuliana's brother, because the daughter in a family must always marry first. It was the way things were done in Mosciano Sant'Angelo.

HIDDEN IN TERAMO

"She's in Teramo; Silvia moved her to Teramo so you can't talk with her," a woman told Biagio, "but never tell anyone I told you," she said walking off quickly.

It was true, Silvia had shipped Giuliana off to stay with her father's sister in Teramo.

There she stayed as a prisoner, not allowed outside alone, ever.

Biagio borrowed a car, drove to the large town, and roamed the streets asking, "Have you seen this girl? She is the girl I want to marry. Can you help me?"

But they did not know Biagio there, and did not tell him the house the girl was in.

He would walk the streets, and look up into the windows, hoping to see her.

But he found nothing.

THE SPRING OF DISCONTENT

Vince would return to Italy in two weeks, and Silvia moved ahead as if they were engaged, but they were not.

The priest had arranged the meeting with Gennaro and Silvia as they needed permission from the city administration for Giuliana to marry because she was just 17, and not of legal age. It was the priest who made recommendations yes or no to the City.

Gennaro felt his tie and straightened his suit, Silvia had on a plain black dress as they sat at the kitchen table of the cottage.

Sister Gena provided them all with a cappuccino and bit of fruit and left the cottage.

"We want your permission for Vince to marry Giuliana," Silvia said very directly.

The priest looked at Gennaro.

"Yes, we want your permission," said Gennaro.

"I don't think you've told me the whole story," said the priest.

Silvia looked at Gennaro; then Gennaro looked up and said, "He's a good choice, he lives in America, and…"

Silvia pushed her thigh against his, but Gennaro continued.

"He loves her and he's, he's…."

"He's what? Providing you money to buy your house? What, you think I didn't know?" said the priest.

Both seemed so relieved he knew.

"He offered the money to help us after we'd decided that it was a good match, not before. He's just helping us; his new family, and the house may be his and Giuliana's in time, so really, it's for them in the long run," Silvia said.

"It may be their home? You mean it may not," said the priest.

Silvia did not speak, the priest always made her uncomfortable when he was asking her questions.

The priest continued, "They are to live in America, what use is the house here?" the Priest asked.

"I will give you my advice…I think you should ask her who she loves. Ask her who she wants to marry. Ask her if she wants to move to America. It should be her decision, unrelated to your personal finances," the priest said.

Silvia was furious, what did he mean, "personal finances?" it was for the family, surely he could see that.

"Alright Father," said Silvia, standing up, "that's good advice." The couple walked arm-in-arm back to the Piazza and home. "I wonder what rat told him, it's none of their business," she said to Gennaro.

Everyone tipped their hat to the two, and spoke words of greeting.

"I heard your concert Gennaro, absolutely beautiful," and Silvia would squeeze his arm and say, "He's a little genius, my Gennaro. He won my heart with his trumpet."

"Is that true?" he asked her on the way home.

And as the couple approached their house with its beautiful view of the Adriatic Sea to the East and the Grand Sassos mountains to the West, they knew it would be theirs, that it was safe, the family home would be saved after all, and that once again, Silvia had done the right thing, the smart thing. Their ship was safe.

WEDDING PREPARATIONS

Vince returned in May from America to find the machine in high gear driving forward to a marriage, just as he wanted.

Silvia spent hours with the dressmaker to make Giuliana's wedding dress, planned the food, and made up the list of those to be invited to the wedding.

"We're just getting it all ready in case you do say yes," her mother would say to Giuliana.

Giuliana was forbidden to discuss what the status of the relationship was, because "It's private between you and Vince, and don't gossip," her mother said.

These things took place all around Giuliana, and often it seemed she was watching a panoramic movie which surrounded her. She was not connected to these events, and Silvia handled everything.

"All these things, but I haven't told Vince I'll marry him," Giuliana put in her diary.

How Silvia was able to keep Biagio away from Giuliana was a testament to her organizational skills and the extent of her network of friends and acquaintances, and their loyalty to her.

THE PRIEST TRIES AGAIN

The priest saw Silvia and Gennaro on Market Day in the mass of hundreds of people, so the couple were not able to see him and walk away to avoid him as they'd done several times.

The priest took Silvia by the arm, "Let's go into the little church," he said.

The small round church was at one end of the Piazza, and was used very seldom.

He locked the door behind the couple and took them to a small office in back.

"I understand you are preparing for the wedding for your daughter," he said to Silvia and Gennaro.

"We will have a civil wedding, but after that we want something in the church," she said, "and we want to spare no expense."

He nodded.

"I know more about your situation than you think I do," he said, "and I don't judge you, only God judges."

"Giuliana will decide if she chooses to marry Vince, just as you suggested to us," said Silvia.

"After you've made all the wedding plans?" said the priest.

"I wonder if you realize what you are doing. You only have one daughter, and she will be in America. She will not be here to care for you in your old age, and old age comes to everyone. Have you thought you may regret this?" asked the priest.

Both were silent, Gennaro looked at his shoes and remembered when he cut the leather, he could not participate as he'd been told by Silvia to keep quiet as it would just cause more trouble with the priest.

"Vince is a good man," said Silvia after some time, "and when they want to return to Italy, we'll have a home for them to live in."

"It may work out that way, that's true, but when you take a choice away from a person—an important choice like who you will marry, then that person's life is not their own…it is something else," said the priest.

The couple's eyes wandered as they looked at the lovely paintings on the walls and ceilings.

A PRIEST'S LAST WORDS

Giuliana had told the priest she wanted to go to confession, but he said, "No, I want to talk to you privately."

So the two went into an office in his church.

She sat.

"Giuliana, I know you are going to get married, I know about everything, everything," he said with an emphasis.

She was silent, her mind was blank.

"The first thing I'm going to tell you is this…America will give you everything, and there you will find everything, but you will never find this sky, those mountains, or that beach," he said pointing to each, "or this air and this climate. It will only be found here."

"My child, really, are you sure you want to leave Italy and go to America and marry this man? Answer me please."

"Father, I don't know what I want anymore. I am so confused. The entire wedding is set. Given everything, I guess I have to marry Vince," she said.

He knew she was marrying Vince for the money to buy the family home, but did not mention it out of respect for her.

"You have a great love for your family," he said rising, "and I will pray for you every day."

SPRING

Vince had returned in the spring, as he said he would.

"All I've thought about is you, and how much I love you. You will marry me won't you?" asked Vince.

"It could work out, maybe I'll care for him more in time," Giuliana thought, "but I only dated him 3 weeks, I hardly know him."

"I can't have my parents thrown from their home, and if I want to come back to Italy, we'll have our own house."

And for once, Giuliana had agreed with something Silvia said: "There are worse things than being married to a man who will do anything for you."

Giuliana sat quiet for many minutes, and nodded, "Yes."

The city administrator who filled out the papers for the civil wedding required Silvia, Gennaro, Vince and Giuliana to come sit in his office.

He was new to the job in town, so spoke very freely to them.

"Do you realize what you are doing?" he asked of the parents.

"You are only 17," he said to Giuliana.

"Why are you letting your daughter get married so young, is she pregnant?" he asked.

"No," said Silvia. "She is a good girl. This is the man she wants to marry."

"Is it?" he said looking at Giuliana.

Giuliana said nothing.

"He has a good job in America, and my sister can keep an eye on her," Silvia added.

He signed the form and handed it to them.

"Good luck in your marriage," he said.

GYPSIES...ATTEMPTED RAPE

The girl came to the home of Honto and Guardia at 1:00 in the morning, driven by a policeman who drove off before even being sure someone was at home.

Guardia opened the door to see her friend's daughter with blood pouring from a broken nose.

Honto came to the kitchen, "What is this noise?"

"Go to bed," said Guardia, "I'll tell you later."

Guardia washed the wound and bent the girl's nose back, which caused the girl to scream in pain.

Alfardo appeared at the doorway, watching.

Guardia looked up at him.

As Guardia held the wet cloth onto her bleeding nostrils, the girl spoke in halting words, broken only by sobs, as blood and tears and mucus poured forth.

"He tried to rape me. He grabbed at my pants to pull them down and touched me when I tried to…then he slapped me."

"Then he punched me in the face until he'd broken my nose, and said I got what I deserved. He called me a whore."

"Who?" asked Guardia.

"Paulo."

OLD FRIENDS

Honto stopped to buy his old and close friend's favorite licorice liqueur, and putting the bottle under his arm, walked slowly along the streets near the Piazza, then quickly stepped into a private alleyway and turned a corner, knocking on the heavy wooden door of a brick home with iron security gratings on all the windows.

Darius looked through the peephole and opened the door, "Right on time, and I can guess what's in the bottle."

The two talked for some time of the new restaurant, and the new officers on the police force coming from Rome, and then Darius, the Chief of Police, said, "What do you have for me?"

"The team is from the Balkans, like last time, and they are bringing the heroin in next week, Tuesday night, in the evening around midnight," said Honto.

"Poison, they should be ashamed," said Darius. "What would I do without you? If only the people knew what you do to keep them safe from drugs, they'd love you."

"None of us want drugs in Mosciano Sant'Angelo—but I don't want the people's love, love comes at a cost, always a cost," said Honto as he opened the liqueur while Darius went to the cabinet, bringing out two small red fluted glasses.

"One other thing, one of your people is on the junk," said Darius.

"Who?" said Honto.

"Paulo," said Darius.

"Thank you my friend," said Honto.

"See, we both help each other with the cleaning, like dutiful women," said Darius with a smile.

And the two enjoyed a discussion with much laughter until two in the morning.

GYPSY DEAL

"I know you love Alvana, I know you want her," said Honto at the kitchen table as Guardia placed the glasses of licorice liqueur on the table.

"But there is something you must do—and then she is yours, and you will then be a part of the family."

Alfardo nodded and leaned in closer to hear clearly.

David E. Kettlewell

GYPSY DARK NIGHT

The truck sat in the drive outside the gypsy house as Honto, the head of the family, told Alfardo and Paulo, "Stop and pick up Gino, he'll help you with the boxes," adding, "I put a tarp in back with the other tools, so cover them and tie them down with the rope."

"I know, tie the rope tight," said Alfardo.

Paulo jumped out of the truck and did as Honto had asked, then returned to the passenger side of the truck.

"We don't need Gino. Paulo and I can handle it alone," said Alfardo.

Paulo cut off Alfardo, "We'll get Gino, just like you want."

The two drove in silence, and Gino joined them, with his massive arms and round face.

Paulo was glad for the silence as he expected a lecture from Alfardo on his date the other night.

They drove in silence, listening to the raspy radio, to a farm far from town, opened the wooden gate and found the house dark.

"What are we digging up?" asked Alfardo.

"Jewels in buried crates," said Gino.

"No one's at the house," said Gino, "just go straight ahead, follow the path."

They went down the dirt path of two truck ruts by the light of the moon, then stopped.

Alfardo lit a kerosene lantern and Gino said, "It's there, we'll dig."

Gino dug for some time, then handed the shovel to Alfardo.

Alfardo took the shovel and swung it hard into Paulo's back, knocking him to the ground stunned, while the two tied Paulo's hands and feet with leather strips.

Alfardo noticed the great strength in Gino's arms, he had no trouble whatsoever handling the lighter Paulo.

Paulo screamed and screamed and screamed like a woman giving birth: he begged, he promised things, told where money was hidden and offered them everything his mind could conjure.

Honto's words were fresh in Alfardo's mind, "Don't shoot Paulo, let the earth take his life."

Alfardo tired of Paulo's screaming and stuffed a rag in his mouth, and tied it with cloth around the back of his head.

"Do you have to do that? Who cares if he cries?" said Gino.

They dug the pit deeper and deeper, it took hours; the ground was hard and they used the pick to break up the hard clumps of clay in the earth.

Paulo was crying the entire time now, even though he had a rag in his mouth.

They shoved Paulo into the hole and began shoveling dirt on top, but Paulo rose onto his knees, so the two brought a large rock and rolled it onto him, shoving his body down with their boots, and resuming the burying of him alive, as Honto had instructed.

"Why don't we just shoot him so we can get out of this pig hole?" said Gino. "He keeps getting up—I'm tired of this shit hole, just shoot him and let's be done with it."

Then again, "This isn't right, don't do it this way, I won't do it," said Gino.

Then Gino grabbed Alfardo's arm.

Alfardo pulled himself free.

"Ok," said Alfardo, as he reached down and took a pistol from a little leather holster on his leg.

Alfardo pointed the gun at Paulo in the hole—then quickly moved his arm, pointing the gun at Gino's head and pulled the trigger.

Half of Gino's head was blown off.

Alfardo threw Gino's body in with Paulo's, with Paulo still crying, and then he covered them both with dirt, jumping on the bodies every now and then.

The cries from Paulo became less and less, and by the time Alfardo stamped the ground with the shovel and jumped up and down on the ground to make it settle, all was quiet, the only sound being the baying of animals and the trees in the light wind.

MORNING

"Where is Gino?" asked Honto at the kitchen table as Guardia sat by his side.

"He was a problem, so I had to leave him there," said Alfardo.

"Leave him there?" said Honto.

"In the hole," said Alfardo.

Alfardo took out the gun and wiped off the prints and handed it to Honto.

"I see one bullet is spent," said Honto.

"Gino," said Alfardo.

Honto reached over and gently touched Alfardo's cheek with his palm.

"You were right, things have to be clean," said Honto.

Guardia said nothing, but looked at Alfardo's face for some sign, then she rose, "Well, let's have breakfast."

She came over to Alfardo and placed her hand on his shoulder and patted it.

"Take a shower, and put all your clothes and boots in this," she said handing him a burlap bag.

The water coursed his body as he looked down to see the dirt and water swirl down the drain. Some dirt remained, so he used his foot to guide it down the hole, until all was gone.

He dried himself with the towel and put the clothes on, which Guardia had left for him on the hamper, and the three ate breakfast together.

LOVE

Alvana came to his room two nights later.

Soft light came in through the window.

She told him to lay in bed and watch her undress.

He lay on the bed naked.

She undid the buttons on her blouse one by one, slowly, slid it off her shoulders, then folded it and placed it carefully on top of the dresser.

She slid the straps of her bra off her shoulders and reached her fingertips back to undo the clasp.

She held the cups to her breasts for a moment, then staring into Alfardo's eyes let it fall and drop to the floor.

Her breasts were small with upturned nipples shaped like little mountains covered with snow.

She unclasped her skirt at its side, slid it down her legs, and placed it on the chair.

He watched her naked body in the light and saw her pull down her underpants, pushing them to the floor with her foot.

She lifted her slender left leg and hovered over him on her elbows and forearms, then ever so gently placed her naked body on top of his, while his hand gently caressed her back and thighs.

"Don't hurt me, be gentle…my Alfardo," she whispered in his ear.

He kissed her lips, and sucked on her tongue and took her earlobes in his mouth, and smelled her long dark hair and stroked it with his fingers while he told her he loved her.

Slowly, so slowly…for the longest time, then he was done.

A small tear came down her face as she held him and kissed him, and for the first time in her life truly felt a man's love.

That morning, he saw a small patch of bloodied stain on the sheets where they had lain, and he knew he was her first.

WEDDING DAY

It was all like a dream—not life, but a dream.

Giuliana saw the things happening around her; the people, the food, her relatives who kissed her and handed her envelopes filled with money, her beautiful dress. It felt like she was in a play.

Vince was so happy, so kind and loving to her.

Biagio's mother's friend, the dressmaker, had a home directly across from the church. He peered at all the wedding happenings through the horizontal blinds.

He saw relatives of Giuliana's, and Vince's relatives and many friends of both: teachers, shop owners, construction workers, and city officials—it seemed everyone had taken the morning off to see the wedding of the Italian girl to Vince.

Two crates of doves were delivered by a white van, the two men carried the crates gingerly up to a spot just outside the church doors.

A small child began kicking the cage with the birds. His parents pulled the boy away by the arm and gave him a lecture.

A young girl twirled her feet one by one, pivoting on the toe while her mother straightened the ribbons in her hair.

Biagio watched Giuliana as she and her entourage walked to the church, climbed the steps and went into the church.

Then the church bells rang and the white doves were released, flying up to the sky and away with Biagio's dreams.

In that moment his heart died…with the flutter of the bird's wings, and with the death of his heart his remaining hope, now extinguished, that somehow, something might intervene…and he felt a darkness like endless night, like the hell of Dante.

The couple walked towards the door of the car, and Biagio peered at her face. Where was the smile? Where was her joy? She seemed so sad.

Giuliana caught sight of the man behind the curtain in the house across from the church as she stepped into the car, "Who could that be, and why do they peer at me?" she thought.

Biagio went to the bathroom and threw up.

EVENING

The party lasted all day and did not break up until midnight.

Every food imaginable had been prepared for the guests who swarmed to the home of Silvia and Gennaro, flowing to fill the large stone patio in their front yard now filled with white-draped tables.

They began with a late lunch, then dancing, and a full course dinner as the sun began to fade.

Chicken and fish, pasta, fruit and wine, all in quantities Giuliana had not seen before.

So many people.

Up in her room the dressmaker removed the wedding dress and the folds of cloth, then went downstairs.

Giuliana looked at the dress and touched the fabric, sitting on the bed.

"Did I wear that dress? And am I now married? Is this me, or someone else?"

The images of the day were unreal to her young mind; they existed only as reflections on the wall, or a film negative.

She felt a strange detachment, and it frightened her horribly because she realized in that very moment, so clearly, that this memory would haunt her all her life; that she did not love Vince truly, not the way that she loved Biagio.

"Why did I do this?"

And her mind thought over all the lies and manipulative comments of her mother and her mother's friends as they held out the life ahead in America, and all the wonders she would surely see.

And she saw that in truth they had spoken of their own dreams and longings…not hers.

How would she live with this realization, how could she live with a man and make love to a man when she loved another?

PART II

TIME ON HER MIND

Giuliana had taken a few months after the wedding to prepare for her new life in America, with her departure planned for February. Her husband, Vince, had flown home just after the honeymoon to New Jersey.

But what she'd expected or perhaps more accurately "hoped" would be a time of joy, was not so.

She didn't know Vince…how could she? They'd only dated for 3 weeks when he'd courted her and arranged a match through her mother, and then months later, they'd had the wedding and just 10 days together on their honeymoon.

The more she thought about it, the more uncomfortable she became.

Giuliana felt a peculiar disconnection between her life and her own innermost being.

She had never felt this way and it upset her. She felt she was perhaps crazy, or ill.

It was as if the life she lived from the moment Vince came into her life, pushing Biagio out, was not her life, but someone else's.

She had become immersed in the world of memories; something typically reserved for the elder years—when one looks back and judges all.

Again and again, she remembered the feelings she'd had at the convent school and how abandoned she'd felt. Giuliana longed now for feelings from years past when the face of the little nun, Sister Gena, smiled at her and doted on all her needs.

"What happened to the doll Sister Gena gave me, with the black button eyes?" she thought. Giuliana could not remember.

More troubling to her, there was an anger inside. It was an anger that grew.

It was a vague thing, and felt like a pot of grey lifeless soup with oil floating on top. Some days it felt like wasps, and on other days like a dry rain.

She felt the weight of anticipation, but no hope, and in its place—dread. What was she frightened of: The marriage? her new life? leaving Mosciano?

"Maybe it's just too much change, I'm probably just afraid for my new life in America."

"How many people had left their homes and come to America from Italy? So few came back, it must be wonderful there."

FLIGHT

Winter in Mosciano might average a temperate 45 or 52 degrees with women wearing light coats and something stylish on their heads, and perhaps light gloves of leather or cotton.

"In America, in New Jersey, it's cold—really cold this time of year," a man from Mosciano had said, and he warned her, "Wear a warm coat, and bring gloves and a hat."

Vince had told her he had his own house, and she was looking forward to seeing it; to seeing for the first time the style of her new home and neighborhood and begin what she knew would be a long process of decorating. "He's a mechanic, I'm sure I'll have to change everything."

Giuliana's family drove her to Rome for the flight to America.

She wore a thick black merino wool coat which went to just past her knees, dress boots which came over the ankle with a one inch heel, black dress gloves, and an alpaca black circular hat. It was a stylish outfit to welcome her new life.

"This all you have?" the cab driver asked when they got to the airport.

"Her other things will be shipped over; she's going to America," Gennaro said as tipped the cabbie.

"I wish you good luck then. People are rich in America, so you'll be both rich and beautiful," he said to Giuliana.

Her mother and father hugged and kissed her many times, spoke of dreams of happiness ahead, and gave her some extra money.

Giuliana had never flown before but was not too fearful of that.

Airline staff were so pleasant and seemed so happy for her when she told them of her new marriage and coming to America.

The flight was very long and trying, and the restrooms so tiny she could barely move.

She slept, and walked in the aisles sideways because there wasn't room to walk normally, and she looked from face to face at the passengers: young men alone, couples, children, and older couples all preoccupied with each other or their plans.

Many men turned to look at her and smile, and each man she passed greeted her kindly.

The older woman with white short-bobbed hair who sat beside Giuliana offered her window seat, which Giuliana respectfully declined.

"Oh I know where Mosciano Sant'Angelo is…it's near Giulianova by the Adriatic Sea. I've driven through it, such a pretty small town. And why are you going to America?" said the woman.

Giuliana pointed to her simple gold band.

"You are just married?"

"Yes," said Giuliana.

"Well, I have been married for more than 52 years, and you have so much to look forward to. Of course, you'll have children?"

"Yes," answered Giuliana.

"They are a great joy, and you'll find your understanding of your own life changes with children. Don't let me go on…because I will!" the woman said bursting out in sweet-sounding laughter.

"Having children is almost as if you are a camera and you find out it was out of focus all along, and things which were not so clear become clearer. Your children are always with you in your heart, and you'll think about them every day, and worry about them too! Oh the years of worry! You have so much to look forward to!" the woman said.

"Your husband is in America?" the woman asked.

"He's a mechanic, and I'm going to see our new home," said Giuliana.

"It must have been hard for you to leave your paradise," the woman said.

Giuliana looked at the woman's hand, with gnarled bumps, discolored veins, and thin skin you could see through and it reminded her of her own grandmother's hand.

She turned her palm to the woman's, and clasped her fingers in hers, and squeezed. The woman squeezed her hand gently back.

LANDING

"We land in New York in 20 minutes, please extinguish your smoking materials, clouds but no snow, minus 5 degrees," the pilot said.

Giuliana was talking with the woman in the seats ahead and did not hear the temperature.

The plane circled the airport many times at a strong bank, then landed with an imperceptible bump and many of the passengers clapped.

When the door of the plane opened, she was shocked, more than shocked…she was in physical pain from the cold.

"I'm in the wrong place," Giuliana said to the flight attendant, "this must be Siberia?"

"No, you are in New York," the attendant said laughing, "It's just very cold today, it won't last."

It was so cold Giuliana could not breathe; her nose was cold, her hands were cold, her feet were cold.

No one was there to greet her when she landed—no Vince, no family.

The babble around her was unintelligible, she only spoke a few words of English.

By asking some 20 people in uniforms she found a man who spoke Italian, and he took her to get her two pieces of luggage.

"Do you have somebody to call?" he asked and she handed him the piece of paper with Vince's phone number on it.

The man made a call, but spoke in English. He appeared agitated, almost mad.

"My dear girl, they wrote down the wrong date, but they are coming and will be here in 5 hours; they have to come from New Jersey and your husband is still at work. Let me show you a comfortable place to sit."

He spoke to a man in an airline uniform who gave her his chair, which was padded and he brought over another small padded chair so she could put her feet up.

"You might as well get some rest," he said, "and I'll find you a little something to eat."

A half hour later he returned with salad and some bread.

"It was the best I could do."

As she looked out the window she saw that there were huge trucks lined in a row, and high mounds of snow.

"What are those?" she asked him.

"What dear?" he answered.

She pointed to the trucks.

"Oh, here we get more snow; much more snow than in Italy, and the trucks push the snow off the runways and the roads."

"Did you bring another winter coat?" he asked looking at her stylish outfit, "and some waterproof boots?"

"No, this is what I have."

"You'll want to get some," he said, "I have to get back to work but will come again if I get a chance."

She did not see him again.

Six hours later, near 7 in the evening she heard her name on the announcement system, and went to an official who took her to where Vince and his sister were waiting.

OASIS

Surrounded by the babble of English, any grouping of Italian-speaking people were truly an oasis, and she was so comforted by the hugs and kisses on the cheek from Vince's sister.

Vince kissed her on the cheek, and was obviously ecstatic to see her. Giuliana noticed the top of his hands were filthy with streaks of dried grease.

"Oh, I didn't have time to clean up, sorry," he said, explaining he'd been working at the shop when the call came from the airline employee.

"You came all this way for us, and we were not here, I can't apologize enough," said Vince.

The apologies went on and on....today's date was given to him by the travel agency but he'd never received a verification, and so thought her flight was next week.

With Vince carrying the little luggage she had with her they went out the doors and Giuliana again experienced the equivalent of an electric shock.

It was so cold—she could never have imagined anything like this. Small, light flakes fell slowly from the sky and landed on her nose and face, melting with a slight burning sensation.

She looked down at the slush many inches deep, she could hardly navigate the mess.

"Here, let me help you," said Vince as he guided her onto the passenger seat, and drove them home.

The car was gigantic, a Ford that was easily twice as large as anything she'd ever ridden in, and the roads were gigantic, and the traffic like Rome.

The sky was covered in a dark grey overcast, which soon disappeared into night.

She had seen the movie, "Gone With The Wind," but she knew their home would be much simpler, "I know that." She just hoped it had some potential and nice neighbors.

Vince's sister insisted that they stop at her home so she could brag to Giuliana about the dresses she was making and the size of her new house.

"Vince, I'm tired, I've been traveling for almost 24 hours, I'm hungry, I want to go to our home," she said.

"It will only take a minute," he said.

GIULIANA'S NEW HOME

Vince had told Giuliana that he had his own home and a good job.

She saw many houses, one after the other, and oddly similar, much closer together than what one would find in Italy.

"It's a city, there are more people," she thought.

They went into a neighborhood with very simple little houses, worker's homes, and she wondered why they had come here.

Vince parked the car, and they started getting out.

"Why are we here?," she asked.

Vince was quiet.

"My mother, father and brother, and me…and you…all of us together…we share half a duplex, there's plenty of room," said Vince.

They entered through a front door to a first floor with a living room and kitchen and a small flight of stairs at the side, with two bedrooms upstairs.

It looked dumpy, not really large enough for two. "How will all 5 of us fit in here?," thought Giuliana.

Michaeli, her father-in-law, was an aged man with a very kind eye which wept on one side a bit, and he dabbed it with his handkerchief. "I'm not crying, it just weeps a little on its own now and then—with the cold," he said as he greeted her with a gentlemanly hug and kisses on both cheeks.

Splendora, Vince's mother, greeted Giuliana in a manner which reminded Giuliana of her own mother, Silvia.

Then a man in his early twenties came downstairs, "Alfredo, come say hello to your sister," said Splendora.

He was skinny with straight foppish hair, in ill-fitting clothes.

Giuliana noticed in the light that all the clothes the family wore were dark, with no fashion sense, and almost unkempt looking. It reminded her of photos she'd seen of Russia—none of the beauty of Italian clothing.

"You don't like something, keep your mouth shut, give it time," her mother had told her in Italy.

Giuliana didn't speak.

"I put a single bed in with Mama and Papa, I'll sleep with them," said Alfredo.

"We have our own room," Vince said to Giuliana.

"There's only two bedrooms, but we make do," explained Splendora.

"Come, let's look at our room," said Vince, as her took her by the arm. Vince patted Alfredo's arm in thanks.

It was a simple space, painted white with an ample-sized bed, two dressers and two nightstands. There was a picture of a ship on rough waters in a badly-worn frame on the wall, and a small green glass vase with flowers.

"I know you love flowers, so I got them for you," Vince said, holding her and kissing her gently on the lips.

Giuliana went into the bathroom with her change of clothes and wiped her face with a washcloth.

She was angrier than at any time she could remember in her life.

"He said he had a home...he sleeps in a bedroom in an upstairs apartment he shares with his parents and brother—five of us in a home just barely large enough for two."

And it sunk in, "They are poor, I'm not poor," and the contradiction to what her home looked like in the idyllic world of Mosciano Sant'Angelo was more than she could accept.

"How was it my parents did not learn the truth? Why didn't they have someone check what he said? He lied to me, he lied to my mother, they sent me to America to marry a man who lives in a duplex rental," she thought.

Her hands were shaking.

She sat on the toilet and cried. She straightened herself, put on blush and fresh lipstick, and went out.

Giuliana stood in the kitchen, but said she was not hungry.

"She's tired, we'll get her to bed," said Vince.

Giuliana hugged her father-in-law and mother-in-law, and Alfredo.

As the couple walked upstairs, Giuliana said, "I don't know that this is a safe time."

"I have to have you tonight, I've been thinking about you, I want you so much," he said.

"When your husband wants you, the only answer is yes if you want a happy marriage," Lea had told her.

When her anger subsided, she fell to sleep. She would call it the sleep of the damned.

MORNING

She had to go to the bathroom, but Alfredo, Vince's brother, was taking a bath and she could hear him humming.

So she went downstairs, and enjoyed a moment of privacy as all were upstairs. She peered out the window to see a much prettier scene.

It was not a poor neighborhood, but middle class, and everyone had a car, and they were all such large cars in bright colors.

The sky was a light grey and cast a soft light over all.

She touched the windowpane with her fingertips and a perfect imprint of frost of her fingerprint remained. The thermometer read 8 degrees, and she saw a bird eating seeds in a feeder.

"Good morning," said Michaeli, and he placed his hands on her shoulders.

"What a shock all this must be for you," he said.

"Well, I'm glad to have to you here," he said, "because I am alone most of the day and Splendora works at the factory."

Splendora appeared, and took Giuliana by the hand.

"I suppose we should talk now, it's best." They sat at the kitchen table.

"We're not rich and everyone has to do their part," said Splendora.

Giuliana nodded, "I can cook."

"No, I talked to the manager of the shoe factory, and he said he will give you a try, I've known him a long time and he's a good man. Maybe you can start stamping out soles, where it's warm," she said.

"You're not going to have her work in the factory," said Michaeli, "She's here from Italy, she doesn't speak English, we don't need the money."

"She will work in the factory," said Splendora, "but today, you stay home and rest, and the dinner should be ready at 5. We have a guest tonight, a friend of mine wants to meet you."

Vince had heard his mother speaking as he walked into the kitchen, "She just got here from Italy, maybe she will work in two weeks, maybe not, let's see how Giuliana feels," he said to his mother with a hard look.

"I'll get something to eat at the factory, they have free oatmeal," Splendora said as she put on her hat and coat, kissed Giuliana on the cheek, and yelled upstairs, "Alfredo, you need to get up, you have to be at the furniture factory in an hour."

Vince said, "Isn't she beautiful, she's the most beautiful girl in the world." He added expectantly, "Can you make some Italian food for us tonight?"

Giuliana nodded yes.

Michaeli said, "I'll help you gather the groceries you need."

A bit later, Alfredo stuck his head downstairs, "Is she gone?"

"Yes, lover boy she's gone, you can sleep a little more," said his father.

"I'm not used to sleeping with two people," said Alfredo, then he went upstairs to nap.

"I'll cook for you this morning," said Michaeli, "and we can make the dinner together," he said pulling the chair out.

"Go ahead, sit down and tell me all about Mosciano Sant'Angelo. I've been there many times, but I love to hear anything of Italy."

And Giuliana told him of her home, and the Piazza, and school, but nothing of Biagio, and the more she told, the better she felt.

She really had never had anyone truly listen to her when she could say anything she wanted, and by the end of the day she adored her father-in-law.

"I'm not your father," he said at the Italian market, "but I can be like your father here," he said as she placed her arm around his elbow.

"Davide, come see the most beautiful girl from Mosciano Sant'Angelo," he said as a small man came from back.

"Oh my God, she's gorgeous," the short man said, "Now you look around at everything here and if you need something else, you let me know," Davide said laughing.

"I mean I'll order it for you from Italy," Davide added.

LIES

She could not get pregnant until one year had passed. Vince explained that this was due to the timing of his insurance coverage at work, so they had to be careful when they did what they did, and how they did it.

As the winter receded, Giuliana found the North American spring tolerable, although the humidity was something she had never experienced before.

Vince had apologized and said he'd never lied about the living arrangements.

"I said we had our own house, and we do. We share it with my mother and father."

"And brother," said Giuliana.

Every other day, Giuliana wrote to her aunt Argentina, and she shared the story of her home arrangements. Argentina had spoken to her husband, Domenico, and they asked that she and Vince come to Ohio to visit them in May for a reception party.

She worked in the factory for one week, but it was disgusting in every way: it was cold, dark, and smelled of leather and curing chemicals. Her father-in-law, Michaeli, saw this and stopped it in a way which reminded Giuliana what a father with authority should do.

"She's not going back, and that's that, I need her help to cook dinner, I'm not a woman."

So she returned to caring for the house and cooking, and enjoying the company of Michaeli as he sang old Italian songs to her, and found a new happiness….dancing with Vince.

DIARY

Giuliana would sit before her diary with the intention of writing calmly, like she pictured a professional writer might do: contemplative and cerebral.

But before long her anger would surface: she wrote in oversize words, then scratched long lines through the sheet, tearing the page or perhaps two pages from the diary in a rage.

She crumpled the pages into balls, kneading them into hard lumps, and threw them in the trash with banana peels in a bag so no one would see what she'd written.

And she learned that not everything can be written.

DANCING

The first time they went dancing at the Italian Club in New Jersey, Giuliana was truly amazed.

Vince was dressed like a fashion advertisement in a men's magazine, or model, in a cream-colored suit with fine auburn leather belt and matching shoes, while she wore a soft blue dress with a flower corsage made of silk he'd brought to her.

He was a man's man, and excellent dresser…not uncommon in Italy, but very singular in America, and the girls stared and spoke of his taste.

He was two inches shorter than Giuliana, but as a couple they were gorgeous.

She was the prettiest girl in the Italian Center, as she had been in Mosciano, with the exception that men no longer stared openly at her figure, but more with side glances.

"You know, a lot of young women here wanted to date Vince, but he said it had to be a girl from the town he was born in."

"After he met you, he never dated anyone. I wish the others were so faithful," the girl told her in the restroom.

LOVE AND MONEY

Her intimate life with Vince brought a smile to her face. He was passionate and could not keep his hands off her, and she felt things she did not know a woman could feel.

"I love you more than you love me," he said, "I know it."

She said nothing.

"You are so beautiful, how'd a bum like me get you?"

She stopped him, grabbing his hair, and looking directly in his eyes said, "You bought me, that's how."

She continued, "You did…you bought me; you arranged to give money to my mother for the house."

"Oh no I didn't," Vince said, "I send the money for the house because they are our family, and I want to help them. It's just a loan, they're going to pay it back or it will be our house someday. I love them just as I love you," he said.

"No, you send them the money because you bought me," said Giuliana.

"Please, never blame me for loving you so much, anything but that," he said coyly.

And she pulled him to her and they laughed.

David E. Kettlewell

VISIT TO AKRON

Giuliana's visit with Vince to see her Aunt Argentina in Akron, Ohio, was one of the most wonderful experiences in her entire life.

The couple enjoyed the bus ride to Akron, away from the house in New Jersey and Splendora's behaviors that more and more seemed worse than Silvia's.

On the bus ride, Giuliana remembered the scene at the house the day before.

Giuliana had worked all day to make Easter bread, and overheard Vince's mother, Splendora, "She wants to take the Easter bread, but I won't give it to her because she's going to see her Aunt in Ohio," then she and her daughter cackled in laughter.

Giuliana walked into the kitchen, "That's ok, Mom, my aunt in Ohio already made Easter bread."

Aunt Argentina had known Giuliana since she was a little girl, and had visited Mosciano and the family's home many times. They both knew Giuliana's mother for what she was, and adored Giuliana's father, Gennaro. There was little they talked of that they didn't agree about completely.

In Akron, Giuliana was surrounded daily by her mother tongue, as all Argentina's friends spoke fluent Italian, although some spoke with a Northern dialect, or a Southern dialect, but living in the middle of Italy—in Mosciano, Giuliana heard and understood all, and they always enjoyed her ability to guess where they'd come from.

The reception party was really the first time an event had been planned for Giuliana that she wanted to attend.

They had a ribbon strung, and recorded music, and food, and dancing, and she had never been treated with so much kindness and made to feel *special*. Even Vince was kinder to her than he'd ever been—being surrounded by a healthy family had a good effect on him.

"I can't believe Vince lied to you about the house," Argentina confided to Giuliana, "but I'll tell you…it was Silvia's doing. But it's also true he's so crazy about you he'd do anything, and you know men. You know men now, don't you?" she said with a wink. "This was Silvia playing a card game, and cheating at it as she always does. I love my sister but she is a difficult woman."

Two days before she was to leave, Giuliana was crying in her room.

Argentina came in and sat beside her and hugged her and stroked her hair, and wiped away the tears.

"What's the matter, did I say something?"

"I don't want to go back," said Giuliana.

"Then don't. Stay here and live in Akron. They lied to you and deserve no consideration," said Argentina.

"No, I will have to go back to New Jersey and Vince's family, but I'll talk to Vince," said Giuliana.

BACK

Back at the apartment, Giuliana's father-in-law, Michaeli, had held Giuliana's arms open, like the wings of a bird, saying how pretty she looked and gave her kisses on her cheeks, "We've missed you more than you could know."

Splendora, however, was in a foul mood and had greatly resented having to take over the cooking and the cleaning and had left much of the laundry and cleaning undone, waiting for Giuliana to return.

"Well, your vacation is over now," said Splendora roughly, and she would leave lists of what she wanted done every day until Giuliana began to feel more and more that she was an employee, or servant.

"She is his wife from Italy, not your maid," Michaeli said.

Giuliana went to her room and looked at one of the letters from her Aunt Argentina, and smelled the perfume. How could her mother and her mother's sister be so different? Argentina was kind and gentle, where Silvia was difficult, to everyone.

"Sit down Vince," she told him the first time they were alone.

She took his hand, "I know you love me, I know that, but I've thought about things."

For a moment he was terrified she would divorce him for lying about having a house, but he just listened to see how it played out.

"I will give you a choice, but I'll tell you the truth—which you didn't do for me," she said.

"I'm not living here; we are not living here in New Jersey with your mother and father and brother in a rented apartment like you did when you were single."

"We will move to Ohio where I have my family; my Aunt Argentina and her husband. We can live with them to start, then get an apartment, which we can afford, and then a house like you promised me, and have our children and raise them," she said.

"Or, I am moving back to Italy," she added.

She was quiet as Vince's eyes flitted left and right as he thought through the options.

Minutes went by and he said nothing. She was quiet, just watching him.

"I have family here; my mother and my father, and brother," said Vince.

"This is not my family, and I don't like how I'm treated by your mother—and I shouldn't like how I am treated by your mother. This is not what I came to you for, and you know that," she said.

She did not move but sat upright looking at his eyes.

Giuliana knew much of her husband; she knew for instance that he was a hard worker with talent, and a wonderful dancer, and that he loved her beyond all else. He was not the most important thing to her heart—she didn't even know what was, but she knew that she was the most important thing to his heart.

"You said you'd do anything for me, and this is the 'anything' I want," she whispered.

For Vince, life was clear and devoid of feelings, or one would say confusing feelings, apart from his love for his wife. He didn't agonize over things or ponder them as a philosopher might, or allow them to haunt him.

He looked at things for what they were, and knew quickly what must be done…if he chose to have that thing in his life, be it a career, or friend.

Vince stood up and pulled her off the chair and wrapped his arms around her, ""Ok, I'll tell you what, if they can get me a job in Akron, we go. Otherwise we don't go, because I have a wife to take care of, and I take that seriously."

He hugged and kissed her, and he felt he was lucky. His wife had not left him.

DIARY

I have a new start…I will go to live with family and will no longer be alone.

My life seems pulled in two different directions; I will miss my father-in-law so very much, he was the first man who stood up for me in life.

He is such a kind and loving man. How will I say goodbye?

And she kissed the page as a remembrance for eternity of the time in her life she said goodbye to her father-in-law, Michaeli, and her lipstick was just visible on the cream paper.

ARGENTINA'S HOME

The couple could not have been happier living with Giuliana's Aunt Argentina and her husband, Domenico—a reserved and genteel man who had many similarities to Giuliana's father, Gennaro, in that everyone loved him immediately.

Vince worked every day and knew his wife was safe and in the hands of loving family, and when he came home the sounds of laughter filled the house.

At night, he found new joy in the eyes of his happy wife.

In many ways, it was the first time Giuliana enjoyed a fulfilling home life, and she savored it.

GIANT AUTO

Giuliana's Aunt lived in a small town called Akron, Ohio, whose skies were polluted with the dark soot from tire factories.

And those factories were run by hard hands from West Virginia, and Kentucky, and from Italy.

Vince had a job the first day they arrived in July.

Argentina had arranged for him to meet Tony, who ran an auto salvage and repair business on Tallmadge Avenue in the Italian district called North Hill, because the road, like much of Akron, had a marvelous hill children would sled on in winter when the cars could not go.

To passersby, it looked like a junkyard, but Vince saw parts.

GIANT AUTO PARTS the sign said, in huge loopy letters of red and black.

Tony's father had started the business, then died, then his brother had owned it and he died, and then it was Tony's, and he was lucky because it made money, a lot of money; he paid so little for junk cars, the parts cost nothing, but he could sell them for two thirds of retail price.

The problem was finding mechanics, and his father had told him this time and again.

He needed a man who could look at some machine; a car or truck, or occasional tractor, and know what was wrong, then tear it apart, put in replacement parts and put it all back together and make it work.

Transmissions made the best money; they were very hard to repair, well beyond what an amateur would attempt, and not every professional mechanic had the knack.

Three transmissions in various states of disassembly lay on the floor of the work area when Vince came in, but the two men doing the work were sitting on crates.

"They gonna fix themselves, right?" said Tony as he pointed to the transmissions as he walked past them with Vince to the small office so cluttered he had to move things from a chair for Vince to sit down.

Vince did not talk long, until Tony said, "I want you to start today, now."

"Let me go home and change clothes, these are my nice clothes," Vince said.

Tony took him through a door to a small apartment.

"No, we have clothes here; my father's and my brother's clothes are in the room through there, they're all clean, and I have boots too, and socks…see there's even a even a private bathroom," he said as he pointed.

"But I need my lunch," said Vince, "I live with my Aunt with my wife, and they will make me lunch…"

"No, I'll get your lunch, lunch for both of us. If those transmissions don't get fixed, I have to give them back their start up money, and I can't do that…it's against my principles."

"I have their money," Tony said laughing, "People pay us money in this business, we don't pay them!"

Tony added, "It'd be a favor for me, so what do you want for lunch? There's a great Italian restaurant right over there," he said pointing.

So Vince called home, then changed his clothes and the black work boots fit perfectly, and it was pleasing that they were broken in and did not bite his toes, and were well-made too.

There were 12 sets of workman's overalls, all clean, and Vince went to the first project, a transmission from a Cadillac.

Tony brought in a lawn chair, and set it close to Vince and watched him work.

If Vince needed a tool, Tony brought it, "The other mechanics said the gears are broken, or bent," said Tony.

Vince just looked at him with a grin, "That's what the other mechanic said."

Vince inspected each component and selected one small part, wiped it off and put it in a paper bag, with a piece of paper with the name of the part and the model of car.

"We need a replacement part," Vince said, handing Tony the bag with the part.

Tony took Vince and opened the back door of the shop, and there was another building full of transmissions, and beyond that, hundreds of transmissions sitting in mud, some covered with tarps.

"Everything you need is here, I have two of this very same transmission, there and there" Tony said.

At the end of the day, the Cadillac transmission was fixed, and Vince had started on a second.

"Vince, take a break…let's take it for a ride," said Tony.

It ran like a new car, "It's as good as new," said Tony with a large happy smile.

"Better than new, because transmissions come out of the factory wrong sometimes," Vince said.

"I'm giving you a raise," Tony said at the end of the day, "and don't call for a ride, I'll drive you home today, and I'll pick you up tomorrow morning."

"I'll bet with a new wife you could use some extra money. If you work 7 days a week to catch up on all this, then I'll pay you double to work on your day off and on Sunday, but you have to work alone on Sunday, no one will be here," said Tony.

Vince nodded, yes.

Tony picked up the phone, "Doc, come get your car tonight, it's better than new. No, we worked on it till it was right, but now it's right. Come tonight and bring that bottle of homemade wine!"

When Tony returned after driving Vince home, he fired the other two mechanics.

"I like you both, I'll give you 4 weeks pay, maybe you should get into body work."

CLOCK

It was Giuliana's 18th birthday, and Vince had waited until evening to present her the gift in their bedroom, placing it gently on the bed.

It was wrapped in white paper with a light blue ribbon.

"To my love Giuliana," the tag read.

"It must be a necklace, or something pretty," thought Giuliana.

She opened it and saw it was an alarm clock.

She opened the window and threw it outside, onto the yard.

"What? No flowers, nothing pretty? You give me an alarm clock? I'm 18 years old Vince, I'm a young woman, I don't want an alarm clock."

He laughed until tears dripped down his face and said he'd get something else for her.

Later, he retrieved the clock from the front yard which he took to the shop.

David E. Kettlewell

DANCING IN OHIO

As in New Jersey, Vince and Giuliana were the best looking couple in Akron's Italian Club, and Vince's reputation for car repair was building.

Giuliana was glad to see that Vince was well-liked by everyone very quickly in town. When he went into a room, people came to greet him and called him a genius as one car problem after the other was brought before him to advise upon.

"My carburetor is not right," one said.

"You let that car sit last winter; I think I told you about that, and the carburetor gunked up. I can clean it for you, as a favor," said Vince.

"You're right," the man said shaking his head, "I shouldn't have done that."

As he finished, another man, Carlo, a hair stylist, pulled on Vince's arm, "There's a shake in the steering wheel, I think the drive shaft is bent because I hit a bump hard two weeks ago."

"The drive shaft is not bent; most likely the tires are out of balance or the wheel rim may have been dinged—but I doubt it. At worst, the alignment got thrown off; bring it over after work tomorrow tonight and I can fix it," Vince said.

And to his credit, Vince worked 7 days a week. When he wasn't at Giant Auto he was at people's homes fixing their cars regardless of the weather, or rebuilding a transmission no one else could fix.

Even the doctors in town treated him with great respect as he was the only one who could fix a Mercedes properly.

"If you'd have gone to medical school, I wouldn't have a job," one doctor said as he squeezed Vince's arm.

When the couple took the dance floor, everyone stopped and formed into a circle and watched them cut up, clapping with the music. True, they were good dancers, but they were also a very attractive couple.

Men would pine for her, and ladies would look at this respectful, muscular man and think, "A man can be a little short and still be wonderful."

THE DIARY...PREGNANT

About one year from the day she'd come to America, Giuliana was sick to her stomach for two days in a row, but with no fever, so Argentina said they needed to see a doctor.

Giuliana was silent as Argentina drove the car from the physician's office.

"You're sure?" said Aunt Argentina.

"He says it's sure," Giuliana replied.

Giuliana lay in the bathtub and touched her tummy. She had so many thoughts she had not had before, and her thoughts were of excitement over having so many new diary entries.

"I was not sure about the relationship with Vince, but now I am to have his child."

"This is not what I thought would happen. I knew I could get pregnant, but didn't think it would be so quickly."

And fears…

"I'm not ready to be a mother; so much is new to me, I just need to get comfortable with where I am but the changes come so quickly."

She thought about her body and how she would get larger. "Where will I find clothes to fit?"

"Will I be in great pain when the child comes? How will I survive it?"

Then she lay on the bed and took a nap.

SHEETS

Before the baby was born, Giuliana decided to go to downtown Akron all by herself.

She had taken the bus with its black foul diesel exhaust smell to the largest department stores in Akron: O'neils and Polsky's—the two being side-by-side on Akron's busiest street, to shop for a new set of sheets for the baby's bed.

She stopped two women in the store, and they were so pleasant to her as she said, "Sheets," over and over, hoping they would grasp what she wanted.

Finally they took her by the arm to the restrooms.

"I don't have to shit, I want sheets," she said in Italian.

GIULIANA'S FIRST SON MICHAEL

As the baby within her grew, Giuliana began to feel that the couple should move to their own apartment, which was a difficult choice because she adored Argentina and Domenico.

They were more than family and more than friends—they were her anchor in this new world.

But Giuliana did not want to impose or even take the slightest chance they were imposing, as it had been 5 months since they'd come to live with the couple, with the plan being for Giuliana and Vince to search for their own apartment.

Argentina had a close friend with a husband living nearby who was willing to rent a second floor room with a kitchen, plus a large attic room on the third floor for a bedroom, so Vince and Giuliana moved.

Argentina and her friend cared for Giuliana through her pregnancy, which proved a herculean task.

After the birth of Michael, who required the assistance of many caregivers as he suffered from colic and would not sleep, with crying non-stop, it was all the women could do to keep things moving forward.

Giuliana was soon sick with anemia and the burden on the two women to care for the baby and his mother grew considerably, but neither woman spoke a word of complaint.

In the days and early evenings Giuliana stayed with the couple downstairs, talking, playing cards, or watching televisions shows which Giuliana could not understand a word of.

Soon thereafter, they moved to another house, which was larger, but only for a short time as they were looking to purchase a home. Vince had paid what was owed in full to Silvia.

In Vince's mind, the payments to Silvia were an investment; "The house in Italy will be our home someday, a home I paid for," and he thought of the house as a second home or investment in the country in which he had been born, Italy.

"I'll have two homes," he thought, "not bad for a mechanic."

DARIUS'S KINDNESS

Giuliana could not believe her luck; A very kind man, Darius, whom Vince had known for years and provided assistance to when the man was injured at work, taking him food and doing errands, had told the couple that he owed Vince for his kindness and would provide $3,000 for the down payment to help them buy their first home.

"I owe you and remember your kind care of me," the man had said as he leaned on his cane, stroking Vince's face.

Giuliana was in the shower when she heard the doorbell. Going down she saw Darius, bent like a statue to one side, leaning on his cane, smiling at her.

"I hope I'm not intruding, I have the money for you."

"Oh Darius, I thought you were coming later when Vince gets home, but how nice of you to come, let me finish getting dressed upstairs," she said as she let him in.

When she came down he was sitting on their couch—as kind a man as ever existed, with a large white envelope on the small coffee table.

"Come sit," he said patting the couch.

She sat to his left and he took her hand, the two facing each other.

"You are a very beautiful woman, and I know things have been hard for you since coming from Italy. I hope you don't feel alone, you have so many people who care for you."

Giuliana was so pleased that someone understood her thoughts, she took his hand and gave it a squeeze.

Darius continued, "You know, money, we all need it, but I am so fortunate that I have so much of it, because of this," and he pointed to his cane and leg.

"I decided of course to help you with the $3,000 for the house, but I was thinking, how wonderful it would be if you had $10,000 more, money for you, Giuliana; something to make your way in life easier…a little secret just between the two of us."

Giuliana was surprised beyond words—she'd never seen anyone extend themselves in such a generous way. At last, the universe had smiled upon her with God's blessing. No words escaped her lips.

"And you wouldn't have to pay it back either," he said as his hand slipped onto the top of her thigh.

Giuliana looked at his hand and with both her hands grabbed and held it.

"I don't know what you want," she said.

"Oh yes, you do," he said as he lurched toward her, grasping at her breasts and trying to pull her to him.

It was a half wrestle for a moment as she felt how strong he was, and then she was free and he half-slipped, half-fell to the floor.

"Get out," she said, as she went upstairs to the bathroom and locked the door.

After hearing the front door close she went down, straightened the table and cushions and saw the envelope was gone.

DEPRESSION

Just a few months after Michael's birth, a deep depression unlike any setback she'd experienced set upon Giuliana like a huge black bird of ill omen; dark, unyielding and relentless.

Unlike a bad mood or being upset, which come and go in all our lives, this had roots down to the very core of her being.

Physically, she felt that she was held down by weights.

Emotionally, she felt like a dried mud flat or salty lake.

Positive thoughts eluded her: She neither laughed, nor visited friends, and began losing weight until Vince was upset beyond words, and for the first time was afraid for his wife's safety.

"There is something seriously wrong with Giuliana, you've got to help her," Vince confided to their friends, including Argentina.

One-by-one, the friends would come and sit with Giuliana, and hold her hand and care for her baby.

Both needed love, both needed care, and very slowly, Giuliana recovered.

But in her memory, it had been like a trip to Dante's Inferno, a personal hell unlike all others which left a scar on her heart.

DIARY

Giuliana looked at the diary but would not take it in her hands.
She would not open it, or write in it.
I cannot say what I feel, I cannot.

BOAT

Giuliana had a small cabin on the passenger boat for her, Michael now age 3, and her new baby, Danny, who never cried, slept all night, and was the exact opposite of Michael in most ways.

She was to have eight months to be with her family in Italy.

As they drove in the car with her brother, William, to Mosciano Sant'Angelo, she felt a part of her come alive again with each landmark and accompanying memory they passed: the convent school; the view of the Adriatic Sea 3 miles distant to the East; and the towering Gran Sassos mountains to the West.

Biagio had been in her thoughts more and more these last few months; what would her life have been like had she married the man she loved… had her parents not torn her from him…had she never left this paradise?

The argument started about the house.

"This house will not be yours, it will be split between all our children when we die," Silvia had countered when Giuliana referred to it as her and Vince's second home.

"Vince paid for this house; his work as a mechanic paid for this house, and we lived not in a home, but apartments to pay for it. It should be his, or ours," Giuliana said.

"It's mine, and that's that," Silvia had said.

"But if you come back to live here in Italy, the house and the store would all be yours," she said to her daughter, "if you don't, we have to split the house between all our children."

THE TWO OXEN

Friends had Giuliana's children for the day, and early that morning, Gennaro took her gingerly by the hand to show her the garden he'd planted.

"See the flowers—what you wanted all these years; what you always dreamed of, all for you," her father had said.

She looked at the yellows and blues and reds, and smelled them, touching each, and some had a lovely fragrance.

But she felt anger, thinking, "All my life I ask for flowers and he plants them when I am gone to America."

She said she wanted to go buy bread and left the house.

It was then, at the bread store, that a woman who will remain nameless came to her.

"We need to talk," the woman said.

They found a quiet street and stood alone.

"You're a good girl, and I wanted you to know," the woman said to her.

Giuliana had no idea what the woman wanted to talk about and looked at her intently.

"A relative of mine was at a restaurant in Giulianova, before you were married, and overheard your mother, Silvia, and Vince. She said he could have you if he paid for their house. She sold you. I've seen a lot from Silvia, but this is too much. I probably shouldn't have told you. I feel terrible doing this, but felt terrible not telling you," said the woman who turned away quickly and walked off.

"No, no, I'm glad you did," said Giuliana, half to herself, and the woman was gone. She'd suspected it for years, but here was proof.

She walked home alone slowly, and entered the house.

"Sit down," she said to her mother and father in a stern, lifeless voice.

The two sat, thinking she was pregnant.

"You sold me, you sold me to Vince to buy this house," Giuliana said.

"That's not true," said Silvia, "who said this, they are a liar."

Then silence.

"Vince gave us the money because we are family, because he loves us, and for your future," Silvia said straight-faced.

And for once in her life, Giuliana spoke from her heart.

"No, when you talked loudly to Papa that day, and I overheard you, you had already sold me to Vince, or planned to. You sold your only daughter, and sent me to America, and he had no home, and you didn't bother to check anything: Did he have a home? Didn't he have a home? He had a room he shared with a brother, in a small apartment his parents rented. How could you do this to your daughter?" she asked looking from her mother to her father.

"You're crazy—that's not what happened," said Silvia.

Giuliana lifted up a book and slammed it on the table and walked out. For the first time in her life she walked away from them.

She heard her mother's voice, "So you are rude to your parents now, you come from America…."

Her mother's voice fading, Giuliana got on her bicycle and rode all the way to Giulianova by the Adriatic Sea.

She wished she could swim, but she had brought no suit, but she saw a friend, and the girl had brought two bathing suits and an extra towel, so Giuliana swam in the water and thought of the time Biagio had kissed her lips on the beach while her mother napped in the warm sun.

She remembered what it was to love a man, felt the love inside her heart and through her entire body, and realized that she respected Vince and cared for him very much, but that this was not the same love you have when your lips burn to kiss another, and when your whole aching heart is theirs, when you can say, "I love you," and mean that and so much more.

When that one person you love is truly everything to you, and a glass prism through which you see all in life, and through which all in life is felt.

She entered the water and thought of what her life would have been with Biagio—with the man she truly loved; what it would have been like to live as a woman in this paradise of her childhood with the sea and mountains and the people she loved so very much.

She thought of the passion she and her love would share.

There was passion with Vince, but one-sided. Vince had passion for her, but not she for him.

How true his words, "I love you more than you love me," Vince had said and he was so right.

These thoughts and more came upon her like dark, comfortless clouds pregnant with rain.

She raised her eyes to the sky and sea, and breathed in the fresh ocean air through her nostrils, with its delicious odor, and thought, "How could I leave this paradise?"

She walked the streets of Giulianova looking into all the stores, and the beautiful handbags and art objects from Switzerland, Germany, and other parts of Italy.

Around 4 in the afternoon she rode the bicycle back to Mosciano.

As she passed the convent school, anger welled up inside her.

"All my life, I've done what people told me. I was abandoned at the convent school and sold into a marriage I did not want, lied to about America by my mother and father, and husband, all to be a dutiful and respectful daughter."

"That the house will be ours is a lie," and she saw that she and Vince had both been misled in their own ways by her mother.

The lies were like a snake that wound around to bite its tail; a circle of falsity leaving pain and tears wherever it slithered.

She was aghast at her decisions, but what she was afraid of most was her own stupidity—how horrible to look at one's life in that cruel way. She saw the errors of her decisions, and saw clearly more than ever before the ways she'd been used…allowed herself to be used.

But she was torn in two, for half of her lived in America with her husband and children, and the other half lived here, in Paradise, in spirit.

When in one place, her heart was attached to the other, yet neither truly felt like home now. Where was home? Where was happiness? Where was peace?

Why must life always be this tenuous spider's thread between our dreams on the one hand, and our real lives on the other?

Why did our hearts and minds engage in this battle of what is—versus our wants and desires—and why the gulf between the two which is like a sea sending ship after ship to the bottom in a storm?

And she remembered a dream she'd had….one night just as she awoke, of TWO OXEN: One pulling one way, one the other—each tied to the same rope; and their muscles bulged and tore and mucous dripped from their noses and blood shot from their nostrils, and still on and on their legs tore at the ground, churning the earth with shaking loins, but each going nowhere…two elemental beasts locked in combat.

This duality; this sensing of two truths which can never be reconciled—both pulling like oxen in different directions—was an emotion she was to feel many times in her life ahead. In some ways it became her harshest reality.

And she sensed her happiness would be like the ground between the oxen; torn and ripped apart by hoofs, and that her life would be a land of struggle and hardship where happiness was only a faint dream from a day long past.

Vince and Biagio; Italy and America; dutiful daughter to sold daughter: opposites—pulling like oxen and the no-man's land always in-between.

But the revelations she had about her life that day…what had been done to her, the manipulation, the injustice, the tragedy even, changed her in some inexplicable way, like a bread whose yeast blooms.

And for the first time, knowing the truth, knowing the lies, sensing the lie, and seeing it clearly, opened a door for her for the first time in her life…to feel whole.

GYPSIES...ALVANA'S TRUTHS

Alfardo's authority had grown since the killing of Paulo; now all the thieves reported directly to him and he reported to Honto under Guardia's eye.

Alvana was now in his bed each night, and he touched her so often and with such pleasure that he knew her body as well as his own; the shape of her entire figure, its taste, the feel and smell of her long hair, her full blood-filled lips to his, and her marvelous white teeth.

But the killing of Paulo and Gino that night—having to shoot a man at point blank range and seeing his brain fly in pieces had taken a toll on him. He felt that he had compromised something he couldn't verbalize; it was a mix of doubt and perhaps shame, but most certainly regret.

"I had no choice, Gino wouldn't go along," he said again over and over. "Everyone must do things, eventually; things they abhor, things they regret. It's part of life," he thought.

And this train of thoughts returned to him many a night, and yes, they haunted him, but always he would remember that Alvana's love in some way cleansed all.

He had taken this pure and innocent girl, and provided her with love and a commitment of a life together, and protected her from all the ills he saw around him.

He had grown closer to Guardia, who now doted on him and called him, "like a son," but more and more and more he resisted the orders of Honto, fearful of the man's violence.

"Why does this man have to beaten? Give him another week," he would say, but Honto would tell him to order it done, and not to think too much. "Let me do the thinking," he'd said to Alfardo, not unkindly.

Honto had smoked too much for too long and he was coughing more, but nothing came up, just white sputum.

A doctor had told him to stop, but he smoked anyway, sitting with his cappuccino at the shoppe overlooking the Adriatic Sea.

Alfardo was so proud of Alvana, and he bragged of her to a thief while they sat on a stone church bench in Mosciano Sant'Angelo.

"She was so innocent, so sweet," said Alfardo as he showed the man a photo of her.

The man with the scar began laughing, "Innocent? She was a prostitute in Rome, I'm sure of it, and my brother had her. She carried her little picture of a baby and held out her hand with coins for money, but for more money still, one could get whatever they wanted."

Had he carried a knife or gun, Alfardo would have stabbed him or shot him, he was livid and his mouth began to foam like a startled horse.

Instead, he began kicking a trash can, kicking the papers wildly and stomping on the metal until it was twisted and broken, and the thief ran off quickly, thinking Alfardo was insane.

Alfardo came in the house with an evil eye and went to Alvana who was drying dishes.

He grabbed her roughly and pushed her into the wooden chair at the kitchen table hard enough where it could have hurt her, but it did not.

"I heard you were a whore, that you whored in Rome, that you had sex for money…"

His voice was rising higher and higher, and his charges darker and darker as Guardia stood with a pistol at the kitchen door, not pointed at anyone, just held at her side.

"Go to your room," said Guardia to Alvana, and the girl rushed out and they heard the bedroom door close.

She laid her gun on the table.

"I thought there was a thief in the house," she said. "So, why do you make this noise?"

Alfardo's head hung very low and spit came out of his mouth as he told her what he had learned from the thief, then said, "But I am sure you will lie to me and tell me it's not true."

"Why would I lie to you? So what stupid questions do you have for me you will wish you never heard the answers to?" she said.

"That she was a whore in Rome," Alfardo intoned.

"She was poor with no food, and no family, living with a man who tried to force her to do foul things, evil things, and she ran away and was hungry on the streets. And she was sent to us."

"She was not a virgin, she said she was a virgin," said Alfardo.

"No, she did not say she was a virgin, I know this. You thought she was a virgin…it was in your head alone," she said tapping his head.

"But the sheet was bloody, our first night…," he said.

"She'd pricked her finger," said Guardia. "I told her to, and to rub the blood on the sheets, because you had to have what you wanted, the way you wanted it…so your dream would have life and you could be happy."

"But you lied to me," he said.

"No one lied to you but yourself, and of all the lies you are told in life, the ones you tell yourself will hurt the worst, and will come back to haunt you most," said Guardia.

"Now, I run this house and everything in it, and I have a gun," she said smiling, "and the gun is loaded."

"And you are going to go into the bedroom and speak gently to her, because she is crying, and maybe you will apologize to her for making her cry, or…"

"You know I could not shoot you, you are my son," she said placing her arm around his shoulders."

"Sometimes love is easy like that first time you had her. But sometimes love is hard because you must love when you do not want to love. That was then…this is now."

She brought him a glass of something sweet to drink, and he stared at the floor.

"Living with disappointment is the better part of being a man, and I know you, you are a man…why do you think we have you in this house? Are you so selfish you will take the only love she's known in life, her love for you, so you can seek a virgin? And what of you, were you a virgin?" she said.

She rose to finish drying the dishes.

He thought about taking the gun to the bedroom and shooting Alvana.

Instead, he picked up the gun and walked to Guardia, and put it on the kitchen counter, and then walked slowly to the bedroom and closed the door to comfort his love, and they both cried tears, but for very different reasons.

GIULIANA

Her father cried that night, "Never speak of what you spoke of today about the money again, I just can't take it, please," he said with his face in his hands.

And she rubbed his shoulder and said soothing words.

She told her parents about the large cars, and the traffic and the cold in America.

"The cold in winter is far more than you could think. It sucks all the warmth out of you, and just breathing makes you cold," she said.

She did not see Biagio and could not ask where he was.

But she found herself thinking of America. What was Vince doing? Was he dancing, and of her father-in-law, Michaeli, and of her husband who she'd learned to love.

Of those who had nursed her when she had anemia.

She thought of staying in Italy, and never going back. She would divorce Vince and live here, but she knew she would never break a marriage vow, she could not.

And he did love her so, she knew that was true, and she almost pitied him that he had lied to win her; but was also proud he had done all he could to win her. She respected that—while she also hated it.

Now Silvia began her new tack which became the mantra for several years.

For within Silvia's heart, she knew she'd lost. Her one daughter was gone, and that fact haunted her each and every day, and every night too.

"We must get you back to Italy, you and Vince. You can live in the house and both help at the store, and when your next baby comes, you and I can care for it together," said Silvia.

"I did not know he didn't have a house; I was lied to also, you must believe me," she said holding her daughter's hand.

Over and over her mother would talk of Giuliana and Vince coming to Italy to live, "I must have my daughter back," she said teary-eyed.

In the late afternoons, her father would pull the shoots from the plants in the garden, or fill the can and water them, roughing the soil on top with his fingers.

He did not speak with his daughter much, and found himself oddly with nothing to say. He would just listen to all she said, and look at her, as if the sight of her would heal him of something he did not understand.

"Papa," she said when they were alone, "Why don't you ever tell me you love me?"

"You have to tell from looking in my eyes," he said.

But the town had begun to gossip about Silvia, saying she had sold her only daughter for money to buy a house, and no one knew where that rumor had started.

Gennaro was respected no matter where he went, but several of the women would simply say hello to Silvia as she passed, and not stop and gossip with her.

Her store prospered and she lent more money than before, on even better terms.

2 years later...

BACK TO ITALY...A THOUSAND CLOUDS

The offer from Silvia to Vince was generous: Come back to Italy and either half the house or the entire house will be yours, and Giuliana can have the store.

Finally, she was making amends for what she'd done to her daughter, and Giuliana felt the spring of hope fill her life like a thousand white clouds held in a perfume bottle.

They could live in the house with Silvia and Gennaro, and that was just the first step to the couple getting the home Vince had worked so hard to pay for.

He could get a job as a mechanic in town, and so many friends had promised to help him find work.

And so the couple had sold all their belongings, except the bedroom set they stored in Argentina's basement. Vince had taken a leave of absence from his new job at Sears, and they were leaving for Italy on a boat.

The hugs and kisses from her friends and relatives in America added to the trove of memories in the diary.

Vince had almost $15,000 saved; enough for their needs, more than enough, for now.

They moved in with Gennaro and Silvia, but soon, like oil opened to find it rancid, Silvia and Vince argued about everything.

It had started when Vince had made a sandwich before dinner.

"What are you doing? I'm making our supper in an hour," Silvia barked.

"I'm hungry, I'm just making half a sandwich," he said.

She took all the food he'd taken out and put it back in the refrigerator, and threw a small piece of cheese to Vince, then threw three grapes on the table.

As Vince ate the cheese his face got redder and redder, and after eating one grape he smashed the two remaining grapes on the table with his fist and walked out.

Silvia scooped them up and said something unintelligible…almost a grunt.

The slide downhill quickened.

Whatever she told him to do, he resisted.

Not one of the promises to help him find a job bore fruit, and as he was not an Italian citizen, work was impossible to find.

"You can't argue with my mother," Giuliana told him time and again, "I told you, she's a Grilli."

"How could you live with this woman?" Vince said to Giuliana, "I am a man, I will not be told what to do by this woman. If I want a half-sandwich, I'm getting one."

Giuliana felt her hope slip away from her like a ship leaving a dock, leaving an expanse of water that she knew would be her suffering.

"If we can't stay in this house, can we at least stay in Italy? Please Vince."

"We'll go North and I'll get a job in Turino at the Ford factory," Vince said.

But now Italy's economy was slow, and workers from other countries were not welcomed with open arms, but were confronted instead with increasing barriers.

The job never materialized as it would have taken over one year for Vince to get Italian citizenship…and he could not wait that long—the money wouldn't hold out.

They stayed at Giuliana's home and Vince would find reasons to leave the house during the day, and spoke little to Silvia, who he'd grown to detest.

Giuliana had felt it coming…like the darkest storm from the Balkans in winter, she'd seen it coming in. Now it was upon them.

"Our money is down to $10,000, just enough for a house. We have to go back to America, or we'll go broke," Vince said. "I will never live in your mother's home again," and knowing her mother, Giuliana understood his feelings completely.

She thought of saying, "It could have been ours Vince…just try again, try once more…" but said nothing.

They stopped to say goodbye to her parents. Vince gave Gennaro a warm hug, and a lifeless kiss to Silvia who stared at him without emotion.

Vince stood staring at the home he slaved to pay for.

He looked at the finely built three-story house, how large it was, with such a beautiful view, but his love for these things was overshadowed by his unrestrained hatred of Silvia.

"There are things which are more important than the house you live in—your dignity, to be a man," he thought, but his heart was wild.

The day Giuliana set foot on the boat to return to America was the darkest day of her life.

It felt in some way like a funeral, her funeral, and she knew it. It was the death of hope.

BACK TO SEARS

Vince's boss at Sears, Thomas, was overjoyed to see Vince back as he had two transmissions which had been back for repairs twice, and no one could fix them correctly.

"You're going to have to get me out of trouble," Thomas said, giving Vince a hug.

Giuliana had come to the shop with Vince.

"This is your wife? I can't believe it," the manager said to Vince in awe.

He actually walked around Giuliana slowly, and then took her hand.

"You are the most beautiful woman I've ever seen, I don't know what to say."

"What, were you expecting a short, fat, dark-haired character from the movies?" said Giuliana, playing with him.

"Your husband, he can be difficult," Thomas said with a smile, "So I think when you die you will go straight to heaven, no purgatory for you."

THE IMPORTANCE OF THE DIARY

When she came back to America, Giuliana felt that the diary was more important than ever.

"My time is slipping away," she felt.

The diary alone was the record of her truth, of what really happened, and the only place where someone could fathom her secrets and feelings, if they chose to do so in the years ahead.

She felt mortal, and for the first time in her life really grasped that there would be an end to her own life, and what would she make of it?

Who would care about the people she'd loved? The pain she'd felt? What she had overcome and what had overcome her?

Only the diary would hold the truth.

So she opened a fresh page and began as she did the first day in the diary, one word and then another: "Our plan to live in Italy was a total and complete failure."

CUYAHOGA FALLS OHIO

The couple found a single-story stucco home in Cuyahoga Falls, Ohio, with the feel of a close knit, small community.

It was a community where people knew each other, and cared for each other more than one found in the larger cities in America.

The Cuyahoga River truly snaked though the terrain, with street after street filled with simple, well-built homes, many of brick.

There was a downtown strip of simple stores, good schools, their own water and utility systems providing both at lower cost than surrounding communities, parks, and quality grocery stores.

Her children would play inside the house, in their small yard, or at the many area parks.

Giuliana would sit in the grass at the park and watch her children play, and she would hold and squeeze them, thinking, "What happiness I feel in life is in these little arms."

Marlene and Eric moved in across the street, and this woman, so similar to Giuliana's cherished childhood friend Lea, became Giuliana's nest of comfort.

Marlene was patient, and caring, and her marriage with her husband was proof to Giuliana that not all in America was sadness.

Giuliana shared her life's experiences with Marlene often, with Marlene listening to each word and offering encouragement.

But Giuliana did not speak ill of any action of her husband, Vince, out of loyalty.

"I live a lie," Giuliana often said to herself as she left Marlene's home with the children.

"I speak of happiness, and I laugh, but I feel no happiness and I feel no laughter."

DR. NIEMAN'S MERCEDES

"Vince, nobody can fix cars like you can, when you were in Italy I was afraid of what they would do to my car—they couldn't even tune it correctly. What would I have done if there'd been something serious?" said the successful physician, Dr. Nieman, to Vince.

"I'll tell you what…start your own business, and I'll provide you the money you need to get started."

Vince shook his head, "No, I don't want the problems of owning a business, I work on the cars, but thanks."

Dr. Nieman asked him 5 times over the years, always receiving the same answer.

"Vince, why don't you take a chance, maybe it will come to something?" Giuliana asked.

But self-doubt and fear kept Vince from reaching forward to many forms of happiness, especially those which put him at risk in any way.

MARCO AND RITA

After Michael's birth, Giuliana's doctor had advised her, "You are just a little depressed, I want you to go to the International Institute in Akron to learn English, you need to meet more people your own age."

In 1972, Giuliana became pregnant with her third son, Marco, and in 1974 with Rita.

To Giuliana's surprise, her parents came to help with both, as they'd sold the store in Italy.

They stayed almost a year both times.

As she held her only girl, she thought, "This girl, my Rita, will not live to be victimized by others, and controlled by people."

"She will have a life, her own life."

David E. Kettlewell

I AM IN PRISON BUT HAVE COMMITTED NO CRIME

In 1980 both her parents, each just a bit feeble, visited her again in America.

Giuliana's father found Ohio weather intolerable.

As the cold weather and grey skies enveloped their home day after day and the snow began to fall, turning the streets a filthy black-grey from the salt, he became disenchanted with Northern Ohio weather.

He would stand at the window and watch the snow drift down in crisp speckles, or sit staring outside the car window looking at what to him seemed just what Giuliana had said years earlier: Siberia.

And he knew he and his wife would return to Italy with its warmth, sun, and beauty.

He knew he would never again desire to see America.

"This weather is oppressive. I feel I am in prison, but have committed no crime."

THE ANGUISH OF YEARS

Once again, Giuliana asked her father to explain how he could sell his daughter to a man they knew practically nothing of.

She understood her mother too well, it wasn't worth asking again, but Giuliana needed to hear an explanation from her father.

"How could you stand by and let me be sold to Vince, when you knew I loved Biagio, and that Biagio had asked me to marry him? What were you thinking; you didn't even check to see that he had a home? You are my father, you should have protected me."

Again, he put his face in his hands in shame, "Please, Giuliana, I asked you before…don't ever speak of this to me again, I can't bear it."

She answered, "I have lived with your actions my entire life, and you tell me to be quiet. Where is the justice in that?" she asked, but he did not answer.

DIARY

"If only my parents and Vince would admit what they've done, perhaps I could bear it better?"

"I know the truth, why don't they just tell me and admit what they've done? Is that asking so much?"

"I need to hear from their lips what they did, what they conspired to do, and perhaps a word of apology for the suffering I bore, and a word of thanks for what I gave them by my sacrifices."

"It won't change my lot, but I need to hear the words."

The refusal of her parents and her husband to admit what they'd done—even though she already knew the truth—was more than she could bear.

Their lies seemed as terrible as their original deceptions; in some ways worse.

Why did they continue to deny her the truth, when instead, her parents could have thanked her for the sacrifices she'd made…sacrifices made for them.

It was like a fire burning, and she could not put it out.

The fire became sadness, and the sadness turned to anger, and the anger to bitterness.

"I have lived someone else's life," she thought.

VINCE'S CHANGE

As years passed and the boys approached adolescence and had their own ideas, Vince changed.

He began to have less patience with their mistakes and problems, spent less time with friends, and began sitting in a recliner in front of the television from the time he got home until he went to bed.

He began a long series of critical comments of Giuliana—an endless stream of criticisms which made her feel he did not respect her views.

"Why don't you admit you bought me from my parents, I already know?" she said.

"I'm not interested in your views on this, or your opinions," he said, "I don't want to hear about it, keep your ideas to yourself," he said.

DREAMS

More and more, Giuliana would dream of her life as a child, and the love she had with Biagio.

"It was so pure," she put in her diary, "it was real love, a tender love."

And she would think about what her life would surely have been in Mosciano, with the warm winters and sea and mountains, and friends from childhood, and her parents.

The priest was right…I have found many things in America, but not the sun, the sky, the sea and the mountains.

VINCE AND HIS CHILDREN

Vince was a wonderful provider, but more and more treated his family with an emotional coldness and criticism which the children and Giuliana increasingly found intolerable.

"Why did you get a B minus?," Vince said to his son, "you can do better."

Giuliana responded, "Vince, he got three A's, why don't you say something positive about that?"

And his children began leaving the house to spend time with friends elsewhere when he was home.

For a woman, intimacy is a sharing of all she is as an emotional being, while for a man it is often an exercise…in exercise.

RITA

"I like him," Rita had told her mother, as they sat at the kitchen table.

"He's kind, treats me well, and I like his looks," Rita added.

"It's your choice; you have to decide who you will love. If you make a mistake, it's your mistake and you'll live with it, but it's your choice," Giuliana told her daughter.

She studied one year in Italy, and chose to live in the dorm when going to college in Ohio.

"I've had enough of Father's critical comments," Rita said.

VINCE'S INJURY & WEST POINT MARKET

Another worker had slipped with a transmission they were repairing at Sears, and Vince was seriously injured.

He was off for 6 months, and to make the money needed for their steady stream of bills, Giuliana had to get a job at an upscale grocer, West Point Market, run by an entrepreneurial genius, Russ Vernon.

There shoppers found a collection of some of the finest foods and chocolates from all over the world. Tour busses stopped so travelers could shop and enjoy the freshly prepared case foods, bread, chocolates, and eclectic beers.

Russ had won every award for retailing one could win; he was courteous to the extreme and arrived at the store at 6 in the morning to taste all the fresh foods which had been prepared. Anything questionable was thrown away and remade.

He tasted Giuliana' lasagna, chicken and vegetable dishes that morning.

"You are the best cook we've ever had," he told her.

"I know," she said laughing.

"If all my employees worked like you do, I would have no problems," he said and she truly felt she was valued.

And for the first time in her life, she had a little of her own money.

David E. Kettlewell

THE WALL—GIULIANA'S LETTER TO VINCE

Her son had asked her, "Why it is Father never says anything nice to us? All he does is criticize…I'd like him to say something nice to me once."

Giuliana had seen an increasing coldness developing in her husband for some time, and Vince's comment that he didn't want to hear her views had hurt her deeply.

When she thought of speaking or sharing her thoughts, she couldn't.

The distance between Giuliana and her husband grew—and she sensed that a wall was coming between them.

So in an act that was so unlike the child Giuliana, whom others controlled at their pleasure, she took a pen and wrote the following to him:

My Dearest Vince Who I Love,

Today is the first day of the new year, 1998.
What I'm going to say to you, you will find surprising.
I've been thinking of doing this for a long time, but finally I decided to act.
The reason I am writing this is for you to know how I feel, and what I feel, because I know if I try to talk to you in person, you will not listen, and you will not give me the opportunity to continue to talk.
You are putting a big tall wall between the two of us.
It gets taller and taller, and the day will come when the wall is too tall to see over and there is no more hope.
Promise me you will continue to read this letter, and read all I am writing.
Please, don't call me stupid or crazy.
These are the things I feel.…

First of all, I want to thank you for all you've done for me and the kids all these years.

I know you had to work hard and sacrifice, but what I have to say is also true and important—a part of the story of our lives together and needs to be considered.

We had four beautiful kids; they are not perfect, and we are not perfect, because nobody is perfect in this world.

You did the duties of a father, and I did the duties of a wife and mother.

We did a pretty good job to have this beautiful family.

And I feel bad because you never have a good word for your children.

You don't want to forgive other people if they say something you don't like. If we go to dinner and they serve a meal you don't like, you get up and leave.

You are a grouch all the time.

Nobody is perfect; each one of us, we have our faults and our problems, but we have to try to understand other people.

Don't try to be so superior to other people all the time. You get jealous when they buy something we don't have. I don't care that they have it.

You've provided us a good home. I'm proud of what you've done.

Our one God forgives everybody, that's what my father always says.

My father used to tell me when I was a little girl that if you get in an argument, you are smart if you are the one to let it go.

You will see that if you try to do this, then you will feel better inside, and you will make other people feel better.

The people around you will appreciate you more, and will want your friendship.

The children want to be close to you but you won't let them. We are getting older, and we will only have each other.

You've said a couple of times when you were angry that you would leave, but you don't want to be alone—an old man alone like some of your friends, do you?

More and more there is a WALL between us, and I am afraid that this wall will get so high we can no longer see each other over its top, and what will we have then, I ask you?

Please think about it.

She put the letter in an envelope on the kitchen table.

It was gone in the morning, but he never mentioned it, or addressed any of the thoughts she'd written.

A copy of the letter was placed in the diary.

VINCE'S ILLNESS

Vince developed headaches, mood changes, then progressive memory loss. The result of the medical tests was far beyond anything Giuliana had imagined possible.

"Your husband has a brain tumor," the doctor told her in his private office, putting a chair next to hers.

She didn't speak for a minute but just kneaded her fingers.

"Can you operate?" she said.

"Yes, we can, but it will only give him a little more time," the doctor said.

"How much time?" she asked.

"Maybe 9 months, at best. Your husband told me he wants to see Italy once more, and I'd suggest you go as soon as possible after the surgery."

David E. Kettlewell

THE LAST WALK THROUGH MOSCIANO SANT'ANGELO, ITALY

After his surgery, Vince recovered his memory and his moods improved. They flew to Mosciano Sant'Angelo, the town where he was born and lived until he was 18 years old.

Vince was so excited that he could remember the names of the streets, and life was a steady stream of greetings from people who knew he would soon pass, so took extra time to hear each word he said, and offer their own reflections.

In the mornings, Vince would hold Giuliana close to him, "I did not tell you how much I love you all these years, how I could not do that? You are the only woman I've ever loved. My own mother was not there for me. Do you know what it meant for me to have you…everything," he said.

"I know you love me," she would say caressing his head, being careful to avoid the scar from where they'd removed and then replaced a portion of his skull after cutting out the tumor.

No one had actually told Vince the exact nature of his illness, and he did not ask.

"It doesn't matter, what will happen, will happen," he thought.

He said he loved Giuliana so many times, and it helped her spirit heal.

But he never mentioned what he'd done to win her, and Giuliana never mentioned it again.

Vince died in her arms at home in America, ravaged by a brain tumor that stole every vestige of clarity from him.

FUNERAL

Vince's funeral in Akron was attended by hundreds, and the stories of how he had cared for their cars were unending.

Mario, a man with drive and energy who had built a very profitable business, Rocco's Pizza, took her aside.

"I remember when my timing belt went out in winter, and we found a torpedo heater and he worked until the belt was fixed, then he wouldn't take any money," said Mario.

"And when my son got married the Cadillac wouldn't start, the starter was bad, and we took the starter to him and he fixed it right then," Mario added.

He hugged her and patted her and told her how much everyone respected Vince, and how Vince adored her, then Mario repeated it all twice.

Person after person did this and Giuliana knew Vince was well-liked, but not to this extent.

MOSCIANO

Two years later, Giuliana revisited Mosciano, and Biagio—married with children to a childhood friend of Giuliana's, was determined to see her.

Through his friends, he followed all her actions, and walked to greet her at the beach in Giulianova.

There was a slight breeze, just enough to keep one cool, and the sky had no clouds.

"Biagio," she said, "You're going to get into trouble with your wife, just for talking with me, and she's a close friend, I don't want to hurt her."

He sat in a chair next to hers, "We need to talk. Why did you leave me?" he asked.

And she explained how her mother had sold her to Vince to buy the house, and all that had happened in her life, her marriage to Vince, her children and of course, Vince's death.

"I knew some of this," he said looking down.

He took her hand, "It could have been so different, so different in our lives."

And they both realized in the fullness of maturity, that it was too late.

DIARY

How many times Giuliana had shared her thoughts with her diary… her innermost thoughts she could not or would not share with another; things so very personal, to be kept private.

The diary…the record of the truth; always and forever, *her* truth.

It was the repository of her losses, her defeats, her emotions which at times seemed to drown and choke her, leaving her gasping for life.

My life…my life…my life…it passes like a candle burning, first some, then some more.

She saw the candle clearly in her mind, and feared it.

"Will anyone ever read my diary, and what will they say of my life, will they care?" she said to herself.

"Even I cannot fathom who I am, and why I've felt what I felt. Was I wrong in the choices I made? Was I wrong to leave my family and home in Italy? and what is left for me now?"

"What is left for me now?" she intoned again.

And she weighed her life in the balance, and felt things she could never share, not even with the diary.

David E. Kettlewell

A LAST GOODBYE TO BIAGIO

Giuliana returned to Mosciano Sant'Angelo, Italy, three years later.

When her parents passed away, the house Vince had paid for was divided into separate living quarters and Giuliana received a smaller apartment on the first floor, with a generous kitchen, small living room, one large bedroom, a bath, and one very small bedroom no larger than two closets end-to-end in length.

Because her brother had traded sections of the house with Giuliana, but Giuliana had not known to inform the Italian authorities of Vince's death, she had a massive financial penalty to pay.

The letter she'd received lay in her purse. It said Biagio was ill, and that they thought he may have had a stroke.

The bell rang, and Biagio stood at the gate.

She had not encouraged him to visit her when she came to Mosciano Sant'Angelo, because it was a small town and the gossip would surely take its toll on their reputations, and she had grown to care deeply for Biagio's wife.

She was annoyed at Biagio's coming without invitation.

"I told you it was not a good idea to visit," she said turning on the kitchen light.

He had come to tell her that he had loved her his entire life, that he had been devastated at her leaving him, that he'd peeked at her wedding through the window of the home across the street from the church, and that not a day had gone by he had not thought of her, and sent her thoughts of love. Finally, he would share all in his heart, all that he'd felt, all that she'd meant to him.

He walked to her and took her hand and tried to speak, but his lips only made smacking sounds.

His illness had left him unable to talk, unable to say a word.

Only the smacking of his lips and breathing could be heard, and the look in his soulful eyes.

Giuliana remembered the words of her father, "You have to look into my eyes to see how much I love you."

He took his hand and placed it on her cheek, stroking it.

"I told you not to come, your wife would not like this, you have to stop coming," she said.

He was so embarrassed; he tapped his watch as if to indicate that he had a pressing engagement and walked out slowly. The gate clicked shut behind him.

"How could you do that to him?" a friend asked later that night.

"This is my hometown and I don't want my reputation hurt, he's married, he should not visit, it would hurt his wife's feelings, and we are friends."

Giuliana went into her bedroom shaking, and wept.

David E. Kettlewell

HONTO'S DEATH

One day at the coffee shop at the edge of the town of Mosciano Sant'Angelo, Honto fell off his chair, dead of heart failure.

The funeral was attended by farmers, friends, and a group of eight police officers and the police captain, Darius, gathered in the distance "for security," but at the captain's orders removed their hats.

Guardia's eyes met the police captain's eyes quickly, and she looked down.

Later at the gypsy home, Alfardo sat at the kitchen table, sad beyond belief as Honto was the rock on which he'd built his life, and the stone on which he'd sharpened the knife of his discernment.

Alvana came in and kissed him on the cheek and left.

Guardia, walked to him and placed her hand on his shoulder, then sat and took his hand as she wept.

"How was it Honto never had trouble with the police?" Alfardo asked of Guardia.

"Later," said Guardia, "I will explain later," she said to him gently.

The young ruffian knocked at the door, and stood before Alfardo.

"Don't carry a knife, or a gun, and don't take everything, or if you're caught you have to go to jail. Protect the family, always protect the family," Alfardo said.

"It's easy for you to say," thought the thief, "You don't take the risk."

But the ruffian said nothing, just nodded and left.

That night, the police chief, Darius, came to Guardia's home and Alfardo was so frightened he thought of running from the house.

But Guardia said, "It will be alright," and pushed them both into a private room where they talked for over two hours, with Guardia bringing in licorice liquor, grapes and glasses.

And after some time there was muted laughter from the room, and Guardia sat in the chair staring at the kitchen cabinets.

THE ROPE TO HEAVEN

Giuliana knocked at the door of the cottage and the little nun, Sister Gena, opened it.

"Father Nicola is tired, but he wants to see you," Sister Gena said.

They kissed and she took Giuliana to the bed where the priest lay.

Giuliana poured out all her truths upon him, and he listened to all.

Of the arranged marriage and her suffering in America, the illness of Vince, and always, always, the pain of her love for Biagio.

"I knew some of this," he said, "that's why I went to your mother with the idea of the convent school, so we could keep an eye on you," he said and Sister Gena smiled upon them.

"And Gena could care for you like a daughter, which she did, so well," said the priest, glancing in the little nun's direction.

"But I have something more to say. I know you did not have Biagio in your life physically, but his love was there for you, like a rope which held you up…like a rope to heaven throughout your entire life," said the priest.

"And this love he had for you, and you for him, was pure and untainted by the stains of life, and be sure life does stain. You had your life, but it was not the life of your dreams. Your life was with Vince," he said.

"Real love disappoints, always, but the dream of love of another never darkens, and it is the only true pure love we know. It was your love of Biagio, and hope, or better said, dreams of something better that helped you survive through life's sorrows," he said.

"Had you married Biagio, surely there would have been many problems," he added.

"Only the love which never actually happens remains pure, it is unstained, and is perfect forever."

She left the cottage and walked the streets, seeing the Adriatic Sea to the East through the rolling hills with their rows of olives and grapes, and the Gran Sassos mountains in the mist to the West.

"I must write in my diary," she thought, and she remembered its worn wooden cover with the Jesus carrying the cross in the center, and the pages full of words and feelings of a lifetime.

CLOSURE

Four years later Giuliana passed of a heart attack in the night.

Her sons looked for the diary for days: in the attic, in the garage, among their father's remaining tools.

"There was no diary," said Rita, "It was just something in her mind, a yearning to be understood, to have her truth known. But of course, it never will be, for any of us."

Rita went into the room where she'd grown up as a little girl, as the men took apart the bed where she'd slept.

As the men lifted the mattress and the springs, they saw an envelope laying on top of one of the thick boards that ran from side to side on the bed frame.

They handed it to her, it had "Rita," written on the outside.

"Why would my mother leave a letter under my bed?" she thought.

She opened the stiff aged pages and read, "Someday, my daughter who I love more than anything in life, as I love all my children, you may find this letter. I will tell you now what I don't think you ever knew. I lived a life which was a lie. I pretended that I was happy, I pretended to laugh, and pretended I was happily married."

"But I have never been happy. I was forced to marry your father, who is a good man, but he was not my choice."

"You know this man, Biagio. The Professor. I was going to be a teacher. Our love was so pure and so strong, I never knew you could love someone so much in life."

"I see my life passing like a candle burning, some is gone, then some more."

"How many times have I wept thinking of what my life could have been in Mosciano Sant'Angelo with the man I truly loved…to have seen the beautiful Adriatic Sea in the distance to the East, and the Gran Sassos mountains to the West, to be in the warmth of this paradise every day… and to have known the tender love I'd have shared with Biagio…and to have felt love in my heart every day."

"What joys I felt in America were felt when I looked into your eyes, my darling children who hold my heart so."

"In your life, make your own choices, you will have to face the consequences of your decisions, yes, but it will be your life."

"I could not tell you the truth about your father and me, it would have been disloyal and I did come to love your father in a way."

"Promise me you will make your own decisions in life."

"I cannot give you this letter now, but it will rest under your head as you sleep."

And Rita thought of the many times she'd been in the uppermost room of the family's home in Mosciano Sant'Angelo, Italy, and looked out the window to view the Adriatic Sea in the distance, then ran to the other side of the room to see the Gran Sassos mountains towering through a light mist.

She burned the letter over a can later that night.

Giuliana's remains were buried in the soil of America, where cold winds and deep snow blanketed all in winter.

Author's note: Giuliana's father had passed away in Mosciano Sant'Angelo and was buried up high in the cemetery mausoleum overlooking the Adriatic Sea.

Silvia, Giuliana's mother, died in Italy, shortly after her husband's passing, cared for by relatives, and with her dying breath said something which eluded her mind and lips until that very moment, "What a fool I was to send my sole daughter to America. I die alone," and death overtook her.

CPSIA information can be obtained at www.ICGtesting.com
Printed in the USA
LVOW10s1043260215

428472LV00015BA/242/P